Some Kind of Friend

MARY FRANCIS SHURA

(Originally published in hardcover as
The Barkley Street Six-Pack)

AN AVON CAMELOT BOOK

Originally published in hardcover as *The Barkley Street Six-Pack*.

AVON BOOKS
A division of
The Hearst Corporation
1350 Avenue of the Americas
New York, New York 10019

First Avon Camelot Printing: December 1992

CAMELOT TRADEMARK REG. U.S. PAT. OFF. AND IN OTHER COUNTRIES, MARCA
REGISTRADA, HECHO EN U.S.A.

Printed in the U.S.A.

OPM 10 9 8 7 6 5 4 3

SOME KIND OF FRIEND

MARY FRANCIS SHURA was the author of many books for children, including *Shoefull of Shamrock, The Search for Grissi* and *The Josie Gambit* as well as a number of mysteries for adults.

She died in 1991.

For Helen and Bart
of
Bird's Hill Road

Contents

1

Number Seventeen, Barkley Street

Growing up would not be so hard if you didn't have so much to do all at the same time. Sometimes I feel like a juggler trying to keep so many things in the air that I don't see any one thing clearly.

It's easy enough to manage pressure when you are little. You can just slam yourself down and start howling. I had just gotten too old for that when Natalie came and taught me about magic. I didn't take to the idea at first but finally I listened to her, figuring that if I even had just a little more power I would have some control over my own life.

But magic isn't the kind of power you can get by plugging into a wall outlet. It is hard and there is a lot to remember. I was not born with a magic spoon in my mouth like my friend Natalie. She must be some kind of a natural. Her world just throbs with omens. She has

1

a little black velvet bag filled with charms that avert doom from her life, and she can chant more scary spells than I can recite nursery rhymes. Just last year she had two or three premonitions, and she had a lot before I even met her.

She even had a premonition the first time she saw me. "There you were," she told me later, "all meek and helpless with that light around your head that they call an aura. I had this instant premonition that I was destined by fate to be your best friend forever and ever."

The funny thing was, I was scared of Natalie that first time. I also was pretty sure that I wasn't going to like her at all. But she was right and I was wrong. We did get to be best friends, and stayed best friends even though she had to move away just before school started this year.

But no matter how hard I tried, magic just didn't work for me. My omens and signs came all turned around so that I got ready for one thing and something totally different happened. And I never had a premonition at all until she was gone and that flash of light came to Number Seventeen, Barkley Street.

We always get a lot of wet weather in October. The rain that day started during Social Science and was still just pouring down by the time I walked home with no boots or raincoat. Since Dad was on the road traveling the way he almost always is and Mom was tired from her work at the office, I took my cat, Carson, and my library book and snugged into bed right after dinner.

2

I had barely settled down before I heard the faint far rhythm of thunder.

When we have storms, Carson goes wild. The black centers of his eyes cover up all the color and his body gets hard and stringy like rubber bands. I snapped off my lamp and held Carson close. From my window I was looking straight across at Number Seventeen where Natalie had lived before her father was transferred to Germany.

Our street looked like melted licorice, the way it always does when it rains. The branches of our crabapple tree scratched and clawed at the house. Off in the sky ladders of lightning rose, followed by thunder that was low and hesitating like the growl of a dog that can't decide whether to be friends or not.

Then a big flash of lightning fixed on Number Seventeen, pressing the image of the house hard against my eyes. In that second, the house became a great wooden person with a tilted roof hat and window eyes half shut with scheming. The scariest part was that something dark and shapeless moved furtively in the shadows of the porch. I felt a dull burst inside my chest and knew, in that instant, that something very strange was going to happen, something that concerned Number Seventeen. It was a premonition! I knew it just as surely as if I had had them once a week all my life.

Then the thunderclap came. My model horses danced crazily along my bookshelf. The wires in my braces jangled, and Carson shrieked and clawed himself loose from my arms.

Carson will never learn about toenails. They work

3

fine for climbing trees but they are worse than nothing on a waxed surface. Carson was still skittering down there on the floor, trying to get up speed, when Mom opened my door and stuck her head in.

"Are you all right, Jane?" she asked, the words coming out quick and breathless.

I tried to tell her that I was fine but my voice sounded funny, too.

She flipped on my light and came to put her arms around me.

"I know that noise scared you, honey," she soothed me. "But it was only thunder."

I could have just nodded my head and everything would have been fine. But I had to be dumb and speak up. My mom is one of those people who don't believe in anything they can't see. She thinks that signs and omens and premonitions are just a lot of bunk. She gets mad if she sees me reading my horoscope in the morning paper.

Without even thinking, I rubbed the place where Carson had left a red streak on my arm and said, "I had a premonition."

"A what?" I could feel her body stiffen just the way Carson's had.

"A premonition," I repeated, already wishing I hadn't even mentioned it. "A really strong feeling that something is going to happen."

"Bunk." Her tone was sudden and loud. "You were just startled by the thunder. The thunder and that cat." Mom is also one of those people who believe that no animals except human beings should be allowed in a house. She frowned at my scratched arm.

My friend Natalie always said the way I give in to Mom and Dad is namby-pamby. Nobody likes to be called names like that, so sometimes I practice talking back.

"The light shone green all around Number Seventeen and I felt a premonition," I said stubbornly.

Instead of hugging me, Mom started jerking at my covers, briskly pulling them all the wrong ways.

"Well." Her tone was flat and cross. "If that premonition was warning you of a doomsday crack of thunder, then it has already come true. Now go back to sleep."

After I heard her door close, I rumpled my covers into a cozy nest again so I could look out into Barkley Street.

Dad used to tell me how he picked out Barkley Street because it reminded him of Donaldson Street where he grew up. Once when we were on a trip he drove way out of his way to show me his old neighborhood. Donaldson was a long wide street with trees so big and old that they met over the middle except where the light company had trimmed the branches back from the wires.

Dad drove along slowly, not keeping in his own lane at all because he was staring at houses and remembering out loud. "That was Step's house," he said. "He threw the meanest curve ball that ever flew by a bat. And the one with the bay windows is where the Palmer girls lived."

"How many of you were there?" Mom asked curiously.

Dad shrugged, still peering at houses and smiling.

"Kids moved in and out all the time but, no matter how many of us there were, we called ourselves the Donaldson Dozen."

"But Barkley is just a little short dead-end street," I reminded him.

He grinned over his shoulder at me. "Okay, we'll settle for a Barkley Street Six-pack. The number of kids doesn't matter as much as how much fun they have together. Surely we'll be able to rustle up half a dozen kids to play 'kick-the-can.'"

But Barkley Street didn't turn out the way Dad hoped. The couples who lived there were older and their children had already left home. None of them had any interest in kids like me except for Margaret Cellini, who was my only friend.

Margaret is as old as any of them but she is different. When Mr. Cellini died she didn't sell her house and move away. While I was growing up, before Natalie came, I used to go over to her house a lot. She played games with me and we had tea parties with gumdrop cookies, and she called me a special name, J.T., short for my regular name which is Jane Todd.

Then after years of being the only kid on the block, younger families started moving in. Natalie's folks were the first when they bought Number Seventeen. We had only been friends a little while when Natalie told me this terrible premonition she had about our street.

6

"Something is going to happen to change everything," she whispered in a spooky voice.

"On Barkley Street?" I asked. "Practically nothing has happened here in all the years since we moved in."

She nodded wisely. "There you go, doubting my magic powers. But you just wait and see."

"Tell me what kind of a thing," I pleaded.

She shook her head with her eyes cast down. "A premonition doesn't spell things out like a movie preview, Jane," she explained patiently. "But I know one thing. Whatever happens isn't going to be good." She dropped her voice and glanced around as if someone were listening. Her eyes glittered as she whispered, "Demons. My private fear is that it has something to do with demons. Up there," she motioned with her head. "Up there at the top of the hill."

I looked where she was pointing. The house at the top of the hill had been empty a long time with a ragged FOR SALE sign out in front, but it wasn't anything like haunted. It was just an empty house because old Mr. Adams had a stroke and left to live in Denver with his son's family.

The doubt in my face made Natalie angry. "Just don't say I didn't warn you," she said with a flip of her dark hair.

When I told Dad what she had said, he frowned a little. "Maybe the house has been sold. Is that what she means?"

"Oh, no," I told him. "This isn't something she knows, it is just something she feels."

Mom heard us and pulled her mouth down that funny

7

way. She didn't like Natalie and made that very plain from the first.

It wasn't more than a week later that the Jarvis family moved in up there with two boys, Gerry and Steve. I thought we ought to go try to make friends with them that first day but Natalie insisted that we wait and see if they were really nice kids or just demons in disguise, the kind she had been warned about in her premonition.

Then the awful thing happened with the kite and that was the end of getting to be friends.

Early this past summer the Ellis family bought the house down at the corner. When Dad heard about their two kids, Tracy and little Mugs, he was delighted.

"Now we have enough kids to have a real crowd," he said. "Maybe we could scale it down and have a Barkley Street Five-pack."

But before long the awful thing happened with Tracy and the ring, and things were back just as they had been before. The Jarvis boys played up at their end of the street and Tracy took care of Mugs down by the corner, leaving Natalie and me together in the middle.

I stared at the front of Number Seventeen. Could a strange feeling of dread coming with a flash of light qualify as a premonition? I hadn't thought of demons or anything. There had just been that dull bursting feeling in my chest. And the moving shadow. I wished I had asked Natalie more questions about the premonitions that she had. It seemed funny that I didn't even know what I was being warned against.

Natalie would have known. But then, Natalie knew everything.

8

2

Natalie

The house seemed very quiet after the storm passed over. Carson was off sulking somewhere and Mom was reading herself to sleep in her own room. I wanted to be asleep myself, but that flash just hung in my mind so that I could see Natalie, plain and clear, the way she looked the first time I ever met her.

Mom was still going to school then, to get trained for her job, but she stayed home summers with me. Since it was August and Mom had time to do what she calls "little extras," she baked a cake for the new neighbors moving in across the street.

She made me go along when she took the cake over to Number Seventeen. It was a white cake, three layers, with orange frosting that had peeling grated right into it. It smelled too good to give away to people we didn't even know. When Mrs. Lowery insisted that Mom have a cup of coffee with her, I was pushed off upstairs with Natalie.

According to Natalie, her premonition about me came that first afternoon even though I didn't like her at all at first.

For one thing, I didn't like her eyes. They were dark and shiny and seemed to be looking at me much harder than they needed to. When she studied me like that I could feel the cowlicks pushing my hair up in funny places and I kept thinking about the pin I had put in the hem of my sundress instead of asking Mom to fix it right.

Natalie was wearing a bright red dress with a whole lot of pleats that you just knew had never needed pinning up. She had thick dark bangs, very smooth, and spots of high red color in her cheeks like a painted doll. She wasn't fat or anything like that but she looked big to me somehow, big and powerful, and I wanted to be downstairs with Mom instead of up there in her room being stared at by such a bright, strong-looking person.

At least she didn't try to make me talk a lot right at first. She started handing me things to do. I unpacked stuffed animals for her to arrange on the built-in shelf in the corner. She stood back and stared at each one thoughtfully as if it were the biggest deal in the world whether the panda was beside the giraffe or over by the owl whose green eyes shone in the dark.

She kept talking while I finished the animals and started stacking games on a lower shelf. By then I was the only one working. She just stood there talking and watching me with those careful dark eyes.

When I set one big board out on the shelf, she jumped

10

forward with a cry. "Not there," she said. "That goes over there on a special shelf."

I handed it to her, a long thin box with a spooky picture on the cover. Big smoky letters formed the word "Ouija."

She stood holding it and smiling at me. "You don't know what this is, do you?"

When I shook my head, she plumped down on the floor and opened it. "It is magic," she said softly. "You can ask it any question in the world and it will give you the true answer. Ask a question."

I shook my head.

"Don't you want to know when you are going to die?" she asked.

I shook my head harder. I only wanted to get away from her. She slammed the board closed with a laugh and jumped up to set it on the special shelf under her desk.

"Everything here is magic," she told me. "These are Tarot cards for telling fortunes. All these books are filled with charms and spells. I have some magic potions but I don't dare leave them out for fear they fall into the wrong hands."

She fell silent and smiled at me in a way that brought lights to her eyes. As little as I liked her I thought I had never seen anyone so pretty. There was such a brightness about her. I was sure that anyone except a shy plain person like me would just melt when she smiled like that with her eyes crinkling at the corners and her teeth showing a sudden white.

"I bet you're good at school," she said thoughtfully.

11

"Not very," I admitted. "I dream a lot, and the teachers always tell Mom that I should learn to speak up louder."

"A lot teachers know," she scoffed. "People don't have to be loud to be important. Some very important people like you are just quieter, more filled with mystery." At the last she dropped her voice as if she had just said a secret.

I was startled enough to look up at her. I had never thought there was anything the least bit mysterious about me and I knew very well that I was only important to my mom and dad, and Carson, of course.

She laughed suddenly.

"Why, you are afraid of me, Jane Todd. I can see right down inside of you, and you are afraid of me. That's part of my magic gift," she confided. "I can see right down inside of people like that."

I really wanted to get away from there bad when she said that. I don't like the idea of people being able to see down inside of me. It was like being undressed when you thought the blinds were down and they weren't. I was afraid of her, and her seeing it made me even more scared.

Then she plopped down on the floor beside me and laid her hand on my arm. Her fingernails were painted bright red. My mom says when I am in junior high we can talk about fingernail polish like that but not before. Natalie was wearing the gold ring with the red stone which later caused so much trouble that Tracy Ellis and I couldn't be friends any more.

"You don't need to be afraid of me," she said in a

really grown-up way. "In fact, you don't need to be scared at all, ever. I'll take care of you."

I couldn't make myself look at her again. I just stacked the games really straight along the edges like they do at the toy store. I was wondering what else she could see in me. Could she tell that I liked to write poems and that I had a whole Dutch Masters cigar box full of ones I had saved? Could she tell how much I wanted to fit in better at school and maybe even someday have a best friend of my own like other kids had?

When the game box was empty I stood up, hoping that I'd hear Mom calling me home.

"We won't fool with that other stuff," Natalie said, leaping up and waving airily at the packing boxes against the wall. When I just stood there, she went on in a persuasive tone. "To tell you the truth, Jane, I just adore talking with you. You fascinate me. Tell me about our school."

What did she want to hear? I started in with play equipment and the carnival we have every Hallowe'en, but she shook her head.

"The kids," she said. "Tell me about the other kids."

"There are about equal boys and girls," I began limply. "There are a lot of really strong boys, and pretty girls too."

"Are the boys bullies?" she asked.

In fairness I had to tell her they weren't. "Just bigger than me," I explained. "But they are all so full of pep, and loud and shiny with sweat and all."

"And pretty girls, you said," she prompted me.

13

I nodded. "There really are. They are mostly really sure of themselves and not shy like me. And they have thick shiny hair like you have."

A dimple flashed in her cheek when she smiled. "It's really sweet of you to say that, Jane. Don't you like your own hair?"

I had to grin. "How could I?" You have to see my hair to understand why her question was so funny. Nobody would like hair like mine. It is too yellowish to be mousy and too dark even to be dishwater blond. And all those cowlicks make it stick up in most unexpected places.

She laughed as if I had said something really funny. The corners of her eyes made cute little crinkles when she laughed and her eyes almost disappeared.

"Oh, but hair is nothing," she said. "When you get only a little bit older, like maybe fourteen, you can wear a wig all the time and nobody will ever guess that you have rat-colored hair that is all tufty underneath. Here. Wait." She wagged her hand at me and shot out of the room.

She was back in a minute carrying a round pink-and-black box.

"Now sit still," she ordered. The wig she fitted on me was a little loose but it was a chestnut color with soft short curls that fanned over my forehead. It felt like a swimming cap in the wrong size. She thrust a mirror into my hand.

"It belongs to my mother," she said over my shoulder. "She wears them all the time. Now, aren't you something else?"

14

The girl in the mirror stared back at me and finally smiled a little. It wasn't that she was so very pretty, it was just that she was so different from the face that usually looked back from a mirror. I didn't recognize my own smile when it came, and something about the face under the rich soft hair looked all those things that Natalie had said, important and mysterious and fascinating. In that mirror I looked like a person who would really have a best friend all her own.

Suddenly I didn't care that Natalie had been rude enough to call my hair rat colored and tufty. I only wanted her for my friend, taking care of me the way she said she would. I didn't even mind her reading inside my mind as long as she liked what was written in there.

That's when she told me about the aura and her premonition that we would be best friends forever and ever.

Remembering that very first day all over again gave me a hollow place in my chest. I felt cold and alone with even Carson off somewhere, his paws probably tucked under his chest, staring greenly into the dark because of the storm. I decided to write to Natalie because writing to her always makes me feel closer even if it doesn't shrink the space a single bit.

I fitted my doll blanket along the bottom crack of my door to keep Mom from seeing that my light was on. Natalie had showed me how to do that when she found out my bedtime was a whole hour earlier than hers.

I told Natalie in the letter how Miss Benson had worn a long plaid kilt with boots and how the older, fatter teachers had glared at her.

15

I told her how Courtney Jarrold had been rushed to the hospital for an appendix that turned out to be eleven bean tacos she had eaten on a dare.

Then I told her about my premonition. I chewed my pencil a long time trying to think of how to get the words right. I didn't want her to say it wasn't a real premonition because I didn't know what was going to happen. In the end I was really honest. I told how the light looked and the way the house changed. Then I described the way my chest felt and told her I could almost see the words "something dreadful" in capitals in my mind.

I really wanted to add some touches, maybe that strange lights had played through the half-shut blinds or there had been some low distant moans, but I didn't. Natalie always said that I would never make it in the real world until I sorted out the facts from my crazy imaginings.

I stamped the letter and put it into my bookbag to drop off on my way to school. Mom and Dad never really appreciated Natalie and sometimes I think they are even mean enough to be glad that my best friend moved away. After I heard Dad tell Mom that I was putting airmail stamps on a dead horse I never did let them see my letters to Natalie again.

3

The Genuine Garnet Ring

That next day I could hardly wait for school to be over so I could go and poke around over at Natalie's to find out what had moved in the dark of the porch. But after school I always have to change clothes and feed Carson, and by the time I got through, Tracy Ellis was out on the sidewalk pulling her little brother Mugs up and down the hill in his red wagon.

I didn't want to be seen prowling over at Number Seventeen. But even more than that I avoid being around Tracy because she always looks right through me as if I wasn't there and never says a single word.

There for about a week once Tracy and I were really good friends. Natalie had gone off to Canada on a vacation with her folks and Tracy and her family moved in while they were away. Our garden was in and since Mom was too busy to cook, she made me take a basket of fresh lettuce and some home-grown tomatoes down to the new neighbors.

I was glad I went because I liked Tracy right off. She was shy like me and really quiet, but when she did say something it was usually witty in an unexpected way. The little boy, Mugs, was cute when you got to know him, and Tracy and he were really good friends. Tracy explained that her mother had very bad health and could hardly ever stay out of bed.

"I've taken care of Mugs since he was little," she told me with a shy grin. "Old Mugs here is like having a teddy bear with a mind of his own."

The three of us played together a lot that week. Tracy always seemed to think of some way to fit Mugs into our games, and when he was napping she came up to my house. It was really great and I kept thinking that it would be even greater when Natalie got home from her trip and all four of us could play. I told Tracy so much about Natalie that she was as excited as I when it was the week for Natalie and her folks to return.

Then Natalie did get home and I found out how little I knew about my own best friend.

I was over at Tracy's house when the Lowerys arrived. Since the car was put away in the garage I didn't even know Natalie was back until dinnertime.

"Natalie is home," Mom told me the minute I got into the kitchen. "She came over looking for you just as I got in from work."

"Why didn't you tell me?" I asked, all excited because I had missed my friend so much.

"I told her where you were," Mom explained. "I thought you would be together by now."

18

The very first minute I could get away I ran over and rang the bell at Number Seventeen.

Natalie's mother smiled at me and called upstairs to her. When no answer came, her mother kind of shrugged. "Why don't you go on up? Maybe she has her door shut."

The door was shut all right. I rapped the second time before she called out, "Just a minute."

After a really long time I began to wonder if I had heard her right and I called out to her. "If you are really busy, I can see you tomorrow."

"I'll only be a minute," she said, and right after that I heard the scrape of the key and she opened the door.

"You'll never guess what happened while you were gone," I began. "The swellest new girl named Tracy moved in down at the corner." I was going to tell her all about Tracy and Mugs but I noticed she had a really strange frown on her face.

"What's the matter?" I asked, hoping nothing was wrong.

"Did you get all the cards I sent?" she asked.

I shook my head, still wanting to tell her about Tracy.

"Not a single one?" she asked, staring at me with her eyes all bugged with disbelief.

"Not a single one," I admitted.

She had been brushing her hair and she laid the brush down with a snap. "That's exactly what my mother told me would happen. She told me all those fancy resorts are the same. You can buy a beautiful card and write on it and stick it into the mail slot in the parlor to

19

disappear forever. Not a single one?'' she pressed, looking at me piercingly.

I shook my head and felt guilty. I had watched the mail every day. I had felt cross toward the last because I knew that even if I was having a super time on vacation I would manage to send at least a card to my best friend.

She sighed into the mirror that matches her brush and comb. ''Well, anyway I tried.'' She paused, and when she spoke again, her voice was lower like it is when she is really unhappy. ''And I had a good time, Jane, even if you didn't care enough to ask me about it. In fact, I had a super beautiful time whether you care about it or not.''

''I do care, Natalie,'' I wailed. ''You know I care and I was going to ask you all about it in a minute.''

''That was actually what you were doing when you came in here all excited, I guess,'' she said in a sarcastic tone.

''Oh, Natalie,'' I pleaded with her. ''It is just that I was so excited about telling you about Tracy and that we have someone else to play with.''

She made a face like something hurt her and interrupted me.

''Please don't say that name again,'' she said firmly. ''I don't know if I will ever in my whole life be able to hear that name without thinking how you didn't care whether I had a good time or how my holiday was or anything.''

I tried to protest and explain but every single thing I said only made it worse.

20

Finally she just looked at me sadly. "Please stop all that babbling, Jane," she said in a quiet way. "I guess I just expect too much from a best friend. Something has really given me a headache, if you don't mind."

By the time I got home I couldn't hold off from crying any more. I was lucky enough to get home into the bathroom and start a shower before Mom saw my face. I cried a long time that night with Carson's sleepy purr vibrating against my shoulder. How could I be such a lousy terrible friend when Natalie was always trying to help me?

Cold at the heart of my guilt was a fear that she would decide that we shouldn't be best friends any more. I couldn't even think about that without fresh tears starting.

I was just lucky to have Natalie for a best friend. Natalie herself could pick almost anyone she wanted to. Everybody liked her except maybe a few mean boys who made fun of her for being stuck-up. I could never decide whether it was magic or not but she really did have some kind of power over people. I watched her at school. She knew just what to say to make people puff up with pride. She had a way of looking at people as if she really admired them. Even teachers played up to her for the look of wise approval she gave them. And she was the only person in the whole world who would want a plain Jane like me for a friend.

The next day when I went over, Natalie's mother said she was overtired from the trip and that's why she couldn't play. Then the very next day she said some friends were coming for dinner and she needed Natalie to help. One thing happened right after another. Almost a week went by before I saw Natalie again and all that time I kept getting more scared and sad because I was sure I had lost my best friend from being so selfish and impolite. I promised myself a thousand times that if Natalie and I could be friends again I would never never never be careless of her feelings again.

Then, just when I was in the very black bottom of the dumps about it, Natalie came over and knocked on our door.

"I can play today," she said casually. "Is what's-her-name going to be out?"

I nearly exploded with happiness. If I had believed in my own magic I would have said I had a premonition then that the three of us would have the best times ever together.

But I would have been wrong.

Somehow when the three of us were all there, everybody changed. Seeing those bright eyes of Natalie's watching Tracy so hard I felt nervous about Tracy. I noticed things about her that didn't matter to me but I knew were things that Natalie had thought were tacky in other kids.

It couldn't have been my imagination. Tracy really was different. All the fun was gone somehow. She was too quiet and almost mousy. I wanted to shake her and say, "Show Natalie how much fun you can be."

But Natalie wasn't any better. It seemed that she went clear out of her way to mention all the expensive toys she had and what a fancy vacation they had taken and how dull everything was back home.

In short, it was a bust.

On the way home Natalie looked at me curiously.

"So that is your marvelous Tracy."

"She wasn't really up to par today," I said, ashamed and sorry to have to say it.

"Well, I am glad to hear that," Natalie said firmly. Then she linked her arm with mine and hugged mine close in that old affectionate way she had before her vacation. "You are such a goose, Jane." She laughed softly. "You let just anyone twist you around their fingers. There aren't very many really special people, Jane, but you are such a sweet thing that you just keep on trying."

Natalie never said anything really ugly about Tracy and the three of us played quite a bit for a while. But it was stiff play. I always felt that I was in the middle and had to keep trying really hard because neither of them liked each other nearly as well as I liked them both.

It was maybe two or three weeks later that the awful thing happened about the ring. Natalie and I had gone down to Tracy's to play because she had to be there when Mugs woke up from his nap. It was too hot to stay outside so we played really quiet inside so Mugs would sleep as long as possible.

We ended up playing with some stuff that belonged to Mugs. It was like clay except not as smooth as plasticene. It kept leaving colored marks on our hands and coming off in crumbs on the floor. After a while Natalie went off to the bathroom to wash the blue stains off her hands.

23

When Mugs woke up we all had cookies with him and then it was time for us to go home. We were already out the door when Natalie turned back with a little cry. "Oh, my ring."

I looked over and sure enough, she didn't have it on.

"I must have left it in the bathroom when I washed my hands," she said. She flew upstairs and it seemed a long time before she came back down with a worried look.

"It's not there." You could tell she was really shocked by the way her voice sounded. "Did any of you pick it up?" We all shook our heads and frowned with her, trying to think where else she might have put it.

Well, there was a great big search. Tracy's mother even got up and came in her yellow housecoat to measure the drain hole to see if maybe the ring had washed down with the water. Finally there was nothing to do but go home without it.

Natalie said she was afraid to tell her mother and father that she had lost the ring because it was a genuine garnet stone that her dad had bought in Turkey and had set in gold for her. But I know she did tell her mom because the very next day Mrs. Lowery talked to me about it.

Mrs. Lowery is one of those people who never seem as sweet as they sound. She would be great if you had your eyes shut because her voice is soft and flattering and very nice to listen to. But when you look at her you feel like her eyes are too eager and watching and you want to look away and your feet fidget.

"That is a very valuable ring, Jane," she told me, her eyes too close to mine. "We may never know what happened to it but you must watch very closely and come and tell me if you ever see it."

"I have never seen it off Natalie's finger," I told her.

She nodded in that wise way. "I know that, dear. I mean that from now on you must watch. If you ever see anyone wearing it or see it lying around anyone's house, you should come and tell me."

I promised her that I would but I didn't realize what she meant until later. Tracy's father offered to pay for the ring but Natalie's father wouldn't hear of it. Tracy quit playing with us right then. Natalie wouldn't go down the street and Tracy wouldn't come up, and that was the end of that. I thought about Tracy a lot and missed her but, after all, Natalie had been my best friend for so long and somehow if I played with Tracy it would be like taking sides against her.

Finally Natalie told me that she thought Tracy had stolen her ring. "I don't think she meant to do it at first," Natalie said. "It's just that she hasn't anything pretty of her own and the temptation was too much, seeing it there on the washstand and all."

I couldn't believe it, but the ring *was* gone and it was gone at Tracy's house and, as Natalie reminded me, Tracy had gone upstairs to get Mugs right after Natalie washed her hands in the only bathroom up there.

But I never could accept the idea of Tracy's being the kind of person who would steal a friend's ring even

25

if she didn't have one of her own. I simply didn't think she did it.

That happened early last summer and every time I see Tracy out there with Mugs like she always is I find myself thinking of ways the ring might have gotten lost.

What if Mugs saw it first and fooled with it? He's just a little tiny kid. If he flushed it away or swallowed it or something he would be afraid to tell anybody. He would have been especially afraid that afternoon with the big fuss Natalie was making.

But it was all over between the three of us anyway, and Tracy has never looked right at me or spoken a word to me for a whole year.

Usually I am not very good at waiting but, as eager as I was to get across the street and check out Number Seventeen, I sort of enjoyed watching Tracy and Mugs. I decided that if I had a little brother instead of a cat I would treat him just the way Tracy treats Mugs. She smiles at him a lot and even when he hollers she just keeps on smiling and does what she can to settle him down. He was swaying back and forth while she pulled the wagon, and you could tell his swaying made it harder to pull, but Tracy just tugged harder on the handle, grinning back at him every once in a while.

The first time Tracy tried to take Mugs in he began to howl and clung to the sides of the wagon with his hands. She gave in, wiped his nose, and hauled him up the hill and back one more time before making him go inside.

The door was barely shut behind them before I was racing across the street to Number Seventeen, hoping that nobody was watching to see me go.

4

The Hiding Place

Fall was coming fast. You could tell by the clouds your breath made in the morning and by how much earlier the sun set every day. The afternoon was already feeling toward dark when I headed across the street. Most of the leaves had been raked away but the last ones to fall had swept along the sidewalk and were piled in wet mounds against the hedges. The FOR RENT sign flapped against its post in the front yard of Number Seventeen.

There were damp circles around the wet leaves on the porch but no sign of anything else where I had seen that dark shape move. I really searched that yard, hunching over to look under the bushes and against the sides of the house and all around the fence in the back. Nothing.

There was only one other place to look and that was the hiding place under the breakfast room.

Somebody before Natalie's folks had added that room

back there by the kitchen. Instead of adding more foundation, they just enclosed the space behind the panels of lattice made of flat boards painted to match the house. To get in there you had to swing the panels inward into the darkness.

I hated that place. I had only been there once, and that was a miserable, awful time in my life. How can you expect a kid to make a choice between a best friend and new strange kids? I had to choose the way I did but I have to try really hard not to think about what happened.

Dad had met Mr. Jarvis the first weekend after they moved in at the top of the hill. He lent Mr. Jarvis a ladder and invited the boys to come down and see us. I was very uncertain when I saw Gerry coming with his dad to return the ladder because I was still thinking of that terrible premonition about demons that Natalie'd had. Gerry didn't seem like anything but a regular boy to me that day and I could tell that Dad liked him right off. The last thing Dad said before he left on his next trip was, "Now you be sure to make friends with Gerry and his brother. It will be lonely for them in this new place."

A couple of times that week I suggested to Natalie that we ought to try to make friends with them. The first time I mentioned it she stared at me in astonishment. "Have you forgotten my premonition?"

I shook my head. "I remember all right but I don't think it had anything to do with Gerry and his brother. He seemed really nice to me and Dad thought so too."

"Let your father be his buddy then," she said with a shrug.

Only because I knew Dad would ask me did I finally get up courage to suggest it again. That time she flared at me angrily.

"Can't you talk about anything but those devilish little boys any more? Are you really so bored with my company? If that is your problem, just go on and have whatever kind of a good time you think you can have with a funny, grubby little boy in handed-down pants."

"What makes you say his pants are handed down?" I asked, astonished. Not that it mattered to me. I have handed-down clothes too and some of them are my very favorites. And mine aren't just handed down within a house, like Gerry's would be from his bigger brother. Mine come all the way from my cousin in Boston who is almost two years younger than me but growing, as Dad said, like a Jimson weed.

"The patches are on the wrong place for his knees," Natalie said patiently. "Why would there be patches halfway between his knees and his ankles and all that turn-up left if they weren't handed down?"

"I don't care what he wears," I confessed. "And I don't know for sure that those boys would be so much fun but my Dad said to be sure and play with them this week."

She stared at me and then shook her head. "Does your dad really think those little demons want to play what I want to play? Can you imagine them in ruffled skirts with big hats playing 'dress up and act out' like we do?"

29

I had to giggle but I didn't bring it up again. She had that kind of warning look that told me she could go off into sulks and spoil the whole week.

Dad was quietly disappointed when I had to tell him that I hadn't played with the Jarvis boys at all.

"I couldn't think of anything they would like to play," I told him, wishing I had stood up just a little more to Natalie.

"Nothing to play!" Dad laughed, pulling me over against his knee. "Why, I could make up a whole alphabet of things to do on Barkley Street."

"An alphabet." I giggled. "You have to be kidding." I love to challenge him like that because then he starts saying things in his crazy fun way.

"Who's kidding?" he said. Then he frowned and began in a sort of stammering singsong because he was making it up as he went along and it's hard to do verses that way.

> "There's apple-tree climbing
> And batting a ball,
> There's catch and there's dominoes.
> Wait, that's not all."

When he paused for a breath I had to laugh at how hard he was trying to keep it going.

> "There's elephant walking
> And frisbees to throw,
> There are board games and hopscotch
> And I Spy, you know."

30

He stopped for breath and I was mean and kept waiting.

> *"There's jumping a rope*
> *And flying a kite . . ."*

"Gerry Jarvis has a silver kite," I interrupted him. "I saw him out trying to get it up but there wasn't enough wind."

"That's it," Dad said, slapping his knee. "We'll take all you little monsters out where there are no light wires and fly kites. You go gather up kids while I find the kite string."

"What if there isn't enough wind?" I asked.

"The difference between just plain wind and enough wind is a kid on fast legs," he told me, nipping me on the cheek with two fingers in a way that looks like a pinch but feels more like loving.

Natalie didn't want to go.

"Weed seeds catch on my socks and itch me," she told me. "I've never flown a kite in my whole life and I don't really care to. What kind of a Saturday is that anyway, to go out and race around and get hot hanging onto a string?"

I pleaded and begged. "You'll have fun," I promised. "You'll really have lots of fun."

"You can go without me if you think you'll have more fun," she told me. "It's a free country."

"If I wanted to go without you, would I be begging?"

She smiled then and the dimple came, but she was

the last one to be ready because she had to change all her clothes.

The silver kite I had seen Gerry fooling with was homemade. It didn't look like much when he unrolled it from between sheets of newspaper, and I was busy helping Natalie so I didn't pay much attention. I was ready to start running with my kite when I heard Dad give a long low whistle of appreciation.

Gerry was racing across the open field and the kite was snaking up after him. It was long and slender with great orange eyes at the top. It slid through the air like an eel through water, rising and rising until it was a shimmering silver banner catching the sun so that it sparkled with light.

"And he made that?" Dad asked Steve, his voice full of admiration.

Steve Jarvis, with his own kite still in his hand, nodded and looked at Dad almost shyly. "It's something else, isn't it?"

"He's something else, too," Dad agreed. "And look at that."

He nodded toward the road where two cars had pulled in behind our station wagon. The people in them had gotten out and were standing, shading their eyes with their hands, watching Gerry's kite dance like a shaft of magical light in the bright air.

Only Natalie didn't seem to like it.

"My ankles itch like fire," she said grumpily when I glanced over at her. "And this dumb kite you gave me won't fly at all."

32

"You have to run," Dad told her. "You really have to run like crazy to get them started up."

"I'll start it for you," I volunteered.

I ran with the kite and got it rising and then handed the string to her.

Once it was up she started running. I guess she didn't think about the strings or anything because she went very fast straight toward where Gerry's tight string was straining from his hand.

Steve saw what would happen first and he started after her. "You. Hey, you," he called.

He reached her at just the minute that the string of her kite touched and snagged on the string of Gerry's. Steve grabbed at her and she went down like she had been hit. I was running with Dad and still I heard a faint sad *aah* from the people over by the fence.

I looked up just in time to see Gerry's kite flounder and pitch and then slither weakly down to drape in the top of a tree.

I wanted to cry but Natalie already was.

She was all bent over on the ground, rubbing her shoulder and crying, "You hurt me. You hurt me," over and over to Steve. Tears were streaming from her eyes and making dark stains on her red shirt.

He didn't apologize or anything. He just looked down at her with his fists tight against his sides as if he wanted to hit her hard again.

"You did that on purpose, you little sneak," he said in a funny, flat tone of voice. "That was the world's most double crumb thing to do to a guy."

Natalie's eyes flew wide as she let Dad help her up.

"On purpose!" Her tone was astonished. "How could I do that on purpose? You hit me, that was all."

Dad didn't speak. She looked at me really pitifully with her red cheeks stained with tears and her eyes brimming. "You don't think I ruined that kite on purpose, do you, Jane?"

I could feel my dad and both the Jarvis boys listening. My mind spun wildly. She had told me she hadn't ever flown a kite. The first time you try things you make mistakes. Why would anyone want to ruin anything as beautiful as Gerry's kite, even if Gerry was getting a lot of attention and I knew that Natalie liked it best when she was getting the attention?

"Of course I don't, Natalie," I sat quietly. "Of course I don't."

Always after that she and the Jarvis kids fought. She said they picked on her and lied so much that it was a wonder that their heads stayed on their necks. They didn't fight with me or lie about me that I knew of, but they looked at me as if I was made of dirt when they saw me on the street.

Later the same summer Dad and Mom and I went camping over a weekend with some friends from Dad's office. Monday morning after Mom and Dad both left for work, I went over to Natalie's to play Fish with her new cards which had black cats on them to give them extra magic. We were just sitting there on the porch floor when I felt Natalie stiffen and realized that Steve Jarvis had walked up to the foot of the steps.

"All right, you little crumb," Steve said fiercely. "Where is my brother's skate?"

She looked at me and then at him. "I don't know what you are talking about," she said in her high-and-mighty tone.

"My brother Gerry got new skates that will go about a hundred miles an hour for his birthday and now one of them is gone. You took it, didn't you?"

She yawned. "I am hardly responsible for your brother's carelessness," she said. "It's your turn, Jane."

I could barely hold my cards much less play because of a sudden ache I had in my stomach.

Steve came up the steps swiftly and grabbed Natalie by the shoulder. "I want that skate," he said fiercely. "Dad saw you up at our end of the street while we were inside for dinner. Now the skate is gone. You're the only person in the world mean enough to take a new birthday skate. Not even your little stooge here would do that," he added with a withering glance at me.

"You had better get your hands off me before I call the police," Natalie said quietly, holding very still with his hand still gripping her shoulder.

Then he shook her and she began to scream as if she were really hurt bad.

Everything happened in a big muddle. Mrs. Lowery was out there on the porch in an instant. She threatened him with lawyers and told him never to set a foot on the property again unless he wanted to be in a detention home. She told him it was a genuine crime to accuse a person of stealing without any proof.

Steve backed away with his face all white until he got a few feet away from the steps. Then he turned and

35

ran. Mrs. Lowery pressed her hand to her head and went inside to take something for her migraine headache. Natalie looked over at me impatiently.

"It's your move, Jane," she said calmly.

"I can't," I moaned. "My stomach aches."

Her eyes were very intent on my face. "You don't think I stole that skate, do you?"

I must have hesitated one second too long because she started gathering up the cards with a cold look in her eyes. "You are some kind of a best friend, Jane Todd," she said sarcastically.

My words tumbled out all in a rush because I didn't want that awful feeling of her turning away from me, and yet my stomach ache was still there, reminding me of Steve.

"I was just trying to figure out where the skate went," I told her. "It has to be gone for him to be mad enough to come up here and accuse you."

Then because it bothered me so much I had to remind her. "I've heard you say more than once you were going to make him sorry for the lies he told people about you."

She stared and drew her lips together thoughtfully. Then she nodded. "I don't know why I didn't think of that, Jane. I'll admit I have tried every magic spell I know against the rotten kid. Maybe one of the spells finally worked on the skate. I sure tried everything in my power, magically, of course."

The thought was overwhelming to me. "You mean you think you might have destroyed the skate by magic or something?"

36

"Without even knowing it," she said. Her voice grew somber. "It had to be that. Why would anyone steal just one skate?"

I had my hand on my stomach which was really cramping. She leaned over and patted me, her face suddenly very soft and tender. "Poor little Jane," she said gently. "I am sure glad these awful things happen to me instead of you. I would just die if someone caused trouble for you."

It was so nice when Natalie was loving. I simply put the skate out of my mind and refused to think about it. Only a few days later the skate was back in my mind, more painful than before.

I was playing Jacks on Natalie's back walk while I waited for her to come out. I bounced the ball too high and it went into one of the squares of the lattice and disappeared under the porch. I would never have gone after it if it had not been my last ball. The earth was sticky in there and smelled like worms. I saw my little red ball right away, but I also saw something else.

There was a book in there all swollen with wet so that it curled and poked up at the edges, and a stocking with a knot in it, and Gerry's shiny new skate.

Maybe it got there by magic. I didn't let myself think about how it got there. Later when Natalie had to go back in, I fished the skate out and hid it in the bushes by the Jarvis house for Gerry to find.

When Gerry started skating again, spinning up and down the street, leaning way over and twirling around and even skating backward where the driveway was flat, I never said a thing. Neither did Natalie, but I have

37

never been able to look at that slimy place again because of the sick sense of shame that comes in my chest.

Now I had to decide if I was curious enough about my premonition to go into that spidery place again. It was hard enough just remembering that first time. I sat there on my heels for so long that my legs ached all up and down. I got up and started around the house to go home.

I was clear to the street before I turned back. I had seen something move in the flash of lightning. I would never be able to settle down until I searched every last inch of Natalie's yard, and the slimy place under the porch was all that was left.

I squatted down again and peered in for a long time. Then I pushed on the lattice and crawled inside. My knees felt clammy right away from the wet ground but I kept on staring until my eyes got used to the dimness.

I saw something light and strange back in the corner. I couldn't tell its shape, really, except that it was lighter than anything around it, like a bundle or something. I crawled over very slowly, watching all the time.

My skin puckers all over when I am in dark dirty places. My skin keeps remembering that black widow spiders live in places like that, and slugs with soft horns. My head filled with a ripe sort of smell like the earth itself had gone bad.

I coughed. At the sound, the bundle in the corner moved and changed position.

5

Stilts

I tried not to breath because of the way the air tasted when I sat and looked at the thing that had moved.

At first I could only see eyes staring at me. Then I realized it was the skinniest little dog ever, with hollows under his eyes like the pictures of people starving. He was pressing himself back into the corner as if he thought I was going to hit him. His hair was tufty and rat colored like mine and he whimpered when I moved my hand even a little bit toward him.

It feels awful to have something little and helpless be afraid of you. Every time I moved he scraped himself against the foundation and cried out again in that scared way. I said, "Puppy, puppy, puppy," over and over until he finally stretched to smell at the hand I held out.

After I petted him a long time he let me catch him into my arms. He didn't fit very well because his legs were all long and stiff with tufted paws.

I am used to the way Carson feels when he is scared

but this puppy was ever so much worse. He stunk of that place, and his ribs were a series of ridges under my fingers. When he trembled it felt as if his insides were all loose in there.

But after a while his shaking got better and he kind of fitted in against me. Every once in a while his eyes would drift shut as if he were just dying to sleep.

Dying. That word really scared me. He could be dying. Maybe he wasn't sleepy at all but just weak. He was too little to go without food and water very long and I was sure that he had been fastened in there ever since the storm. But who was going to feed him, anyway? He didn't have dog tags on or even a collar. He was a really truly stray dog.

I couldn't take him home. My mom is so anti-animal that I only got Kit Carson after years of pleading and Dad finally putting his foot down. And Carson would never let a stray dog stay around. Carson chases off every animal that even gets close to his property. He chased off a big Lab one day while the dog's owner was watching.

"Well," the man said, laughing. "There goes his title as Cat-killer of the Western World."

It wouldn't do any good just to take the puppy out and let him loose. The animal-refuge truck would pick him up as sure as anything. After three days they put dogs to sleep if nobody claims them.

And who would adopt this puppy? He was as skinny and funny looking as I am, and on top of that he had those big long stilts of legs that didn't fit at all. But I couldn't stand to think about his dying.

40

Then I got my great idea. Even though the Lowery house had been up for rent ever since Natalie left, nobody had taken it. I heard Dad tell Mom that it would never be rented because the Lowerys had made a rule of no children, no pets. "Who is going to pay heat bills on a big place like that without having a bunch of kids to enjoy it?" Dad had asked.

If the house was never going to be rented I could just use that space behind the lattice as a dog pen. It was not what I would have chosen, but he would be safe and nobody would ever suspect he was there because nobody ever came around the back yard.

Every day I would bring him water and food and brush his coat to make it silky. I could exercise him in the back yard that you can't even see from the street. He would be safe all the time he was getting plump and sleek.

And when he was all grown and fine and beautiful I would buy a rich, brown-colored leather strap to match his eyes and find a good home for him. Somebody would be as glad to have him as I was to get Carson for my very own to love and spoil.

I knew I was letting my imagination run away with me the way Natalie always said I did, but my plan was possible. I could just see Stilts (that had to be his name) fat and shiny and proud on a leash just like a show dog.

But in the meantime he was starving.

When I left, Stilts was pressing his nose against the lattice and whining to go with me. I had to work fast because it was getting late.

Carson has only one water dish so I had to borrow

41

one of Mom's cake pans. She wasn't likely to miss it since she bakes so seldom since she started working. I filled a sandwich bag full of Carson's food, which is tiny little dry stuff. I would have taken some canned food but Mom counts it off by the week and I was sure she would miss that.

I barely made it back into the shadow of the hedge that separates Natalie's old house from Margaret Cellini's yard when I saw Mom's car turn into our drive. Hurrying made me really awkward. I spilled water all over myself and Stilts before I got the pan settled in there.

When I got out the food, Stilts's shyness disappeared. He just started to bolt it down, not even taking time to taste it. The way he ate scared me. I had read of people getting sick from eating too much after they have been starved so I held back some of the food. Stilts pressed to follow me when I started out so I threw the rest of the food on the ground in there and shut the lattice behind me while he was nuzzling around picking it up.

Because Dad is gone all week and Mom is away during the day, Mom and I always visit while she fixes our dinner. She was breading pork chops when I came in, dipping them first into beaten egg and then into scrunched-up cracker crumbs. When she had slid the last chop, hissing, into the heated oil, she smiled over at me.

"I missed you, honey," she said. "I was beginning to think about worrying."

"I was just across the street," I told her, not wanting to lie unless I had to.

42

"Oh," she said lifting the corner of a chop to peek in under to see if it was the right color yet. "At Mrs. Cellini's? I know she was glad to see you."

Mom calls Margaret Mrs. Cellini because Margaret is old enough to be Mom's mother. I call her Margaret because she tells me to. Margaret is old but not worn out at all. She grows a big garden every year and hoes the rows herself. She even mows her own lawn, wearing funny cut-off slacks above ankle socks. She sings very loud and off key when she cooks as if she weren't all the way grown up, much less old.

Natalie said that Margaret is common because she ties a rag around her head and drags a chair from one window to the other to wash windows. I think that is clever, myself. Ladders are easy to fall from and old people break really easy. I never said it to Natalie but I don't think that Margaret has enough leftover money to hire people to do her work like the Lowerys always did.

"I didn't go to Margaret's," I told Mom, shading the truth just that little bit. "I saw you coming and came on home."

Lucky for me that Mom's mind was on draining the chops and getting cold applesauce out to go with them. "Well, there will be other afternoons," she said mildly.

Mom was right about the other afternoons. The days came and went swiftly because I had my time with Stilts to look forward to. For the first time since Natalie left I was too busy and happy to be lonesome. I bought a big sack of dog food and put it into my closet. Carson

43

smelled it right away so that I had to be careful to shut the door.

Mom smelled it too. She was changing the linen on my bed when I saw her sniff the air curiously.

"Something smells weird in here," she said darkly. "Is it that cat?"

I had my seashell collection out to find some small cockleshells for a school project. I saw her look at it suspiciously. Then she pulled up my bedskirt and found a great wad of dirty clothes under there. She gave me a daggered look as she carried them away, and I sighed with relief.

Mom could have run a quick search in the closet and I would never have been able to explain. As it is, she has long since given up hope of making me tidy. "You're half pack rat like your father," she told me tartly. "Your husband can train you, and I wish him better luck than I have had with him."

Those were such happy, happy days. Stilts filled out before my very eyes. He really liked the bed I made from old bath towels which he could chew on with his sharp new teeth. He didn't look like any dog I had ever seen before, but I was sure that when he grew up to his legs (and maybe his feet and his ears) he would be so beautiful that people would fight over who got to have him for their very own.

Every day when I got there Stilts was so glad to see me that we would just hug and wrestle. Then he would lean hard against me and I would hold him close. I loved him so much that I hurt inside and tears came to my eyes from happiness. He seemed so helpless and breakable with his heart beating so fast and hard against my arms.

But he was really strong. After I fed him we always played in Natalie's back yard. Sometimes I threw sticks for him to bring back but best of all we made a game called Circles.

I would stand in the middle of the yard and whisper in the fiercest voice I could make, "I'm going to get you." Stilts would put his head down between his paws with his tail end way high and wagging all the time because he liked the game so much. I would wait a long time and not move. His eyes never left mine, but he trembled all over from waiting.

Then I would dart at him. He would start to run and race around the yard, around and around in such fast circles that my head spun from watching him. His tongue flowed back like Dad's tie does when he runs, and his ears looked stiff in the wind. When he got tired he would just stop and come over to lean against me, all out of breath and soft again.

I knew already that Stilts would never make a good watchdog. He almost never barked. He had a language of his own, soft whimpers and a low teasing growl when he was playful, and a begging whine that got him lots more dog biscuits than I meant him to have. But he simply wasn't a barking dog, which was really convenient with him hidden away like that.

Those good afternoons turned into weeks. October went and November came with colder winds and little shining slivers of ice in the puddles along the street. At first I worried that the colder days would be hard on

Stilts, but he came so warmly into my arms every evening that I felt he was comfortable.

In school, we did a report on the Incas and I added a poem I wrote and got an "A, Very good" in Miss Benson's handwriting. I made a picture frame in Art and sanded it and decorated it with cockleshells from my collection. We studied similes in Language and I practiced using them in my letters to Natalie.

Natalie and I made promises about writing each other the day I found out about her moving. One day everything had been just the same and the next she told me they were leaving.

"It's a transfer to Germany," she said. "Probably for about four years."

I stared at her. Four years was only forever with the ends trimmed off a little. And the move was only a week away. I hurt inside. They must have known it was coming and she had just kept it from me to throw like a bomb and tear me all apart.

"Don't look at me like that," she complained. "I kept trying to think of a way to tell you, and the time just slipped up on me. I knew something tragic was going to happen. There were all kinds of evil omens, and I have had dark, terrible dreams. I knew something dreadful would befall but I never thought of this. Leaving my best friend in all the world is tragic, simply tragic." All the time she talked she was stuffing dolls briskly into a box.

I sat there with my skin feeling hard and numb like it does when you have been slapped.

"It's not the end of the world, Jane," she said firmly.

46

"We are coming back. We are renting the house instead of selling it. Now would we do that if we didn't mean to come back?"

She stared at me so fiercely that I didn't dare disagree.

"I'll miss you," I finally said.

"And I'll miss you," she said, leaning over to grab me for a hug. "I'll be desolate, absolutely desolate. I'll probably cry my eyes out and get very thin from not being able to eat anything from loneliness."

Something turned in my mind. It would be silly to argue with her, but Natalie never cried in her life that I ever saw but two times. Once she was trying to get something out of her dad, and the other time was the day that Gerry Jarvis' kite got ruined and Steve ran into her out there.

"And anyway I'll write every day," she said in a bright, excited tone. "And you must write me every day. Promise."

Of course I promised and I kept the promise for a whole long time and still got only one card and two letters back. Then I started writing to her only when I was lonesome and only mailing letters when I had extra money for stamps because they charge by the half ounce and letters cost the same to send as a double dip of ice cream in a sugar cone.

But I didn't say anything to Natalie about Stilts. I could never predict how she might react to things. I was afraid she would call me a "Bleeding heart" like she had when I rescued the field mouse from Carson and cried when it went on and died anyway.

47

Once in a while a letter came from Natalie in that square red envelope she always uses. It was hard to get very interested in the stuff she wrote about. She was going to English School and all the kids were stuck-up or drippy and not our kind. They had uniforms, though, with red vests that were just perfect for her vivid coloring.

Because it took almost all of my allowance to buy food for Stilts, I didn't mail any letters for a long time.

After all, I had promised to write every day but I hadn't promised anything about mailing the letters, and Stilts was such a good eater that he had what my dad calls a hollow leg. Or maybe four of them.

6

The Battered Yellow Van

I always like the second Friday of every month because it is like an adventure. When I leave school I have to get on the city bus and go clear across town to my orthodontist's office. I usually don't get back home until almost dark but I don't mind. Dr. Robles is nice and his hands taste like cloves. He looks into my mouth with an eager, excited look as if he is expecting a surprise. Sometimes, when my jaws are aching, I think of things it would be fun to write on my teeth, like "Hi, Doc," or some tiny little picture that he could only figure out with his magnifying glass.

He had told me that "next time" he might be able to take my bands off. Unless you have had bands on your braces you can't imagine how exciting that promise is.

Bands are tiny little rubber bands that look like swollen pieces of macaroni only flatter.

When the doctor puts the bands in, he makes it seem

easier than anything. Then he pats you on the shoulder and tells you to take them out only when you eat. You go off home wondering why other kids complain so much about bands when anybody can see there is nothing to it.

Then you learn.

In the first place they don't go in that easily for anyone but the doctor. I always manage to snap them so that they hit me on the lip and leave a sore place that swells up black. Then I forget to take them out when Mom calls ''Dinner.'' If I excuse myself after Grace is said, I get a lecture on forgetfulness. If I as much as raise a thumbnail to take them out at the table, I get landed on with both lungs.

I had a long talk with Dad about me and Mom and the bands but he sided with Mom, even though he laughed a little. ''Face it, Jane,'' he told me, his eyes twinkling in spite of his serious tone. ''Nobody wants to eat with a kid who looks as if she were performing a home tonsillectomy.''

Carson sits in my window while I dress for school. He was in my window that particular Friday morning, staring into the street and doing that round thing cats do. He had his tail curled all about his body with his feet hidden in under his chest. With his chin down, even the top of his head was as round as an orange. I reached over to hug him for being so cute and nearly fell flat on my bed.

There was something parked in the driveway of Number Seventeen. I got up on my knees to see better. It

50

was a van, a battered yellow van with covered-up windows so I couldn't see what was inside.

Mom was yelling that my French toast was ready so I hurried in and naturally forgot to take my bands out.

Mom holds her coffee cup halfway to her lips when she reads the financial page of the paper. She frowns at the columns of print and flicks her eyes sideways and then up and down with her coffee cup still halfway to her mouth.

"There's a van over at Natalie's," I told her.

"Maybe somebody is moving in," she suggested, still looking at her paper.

"It's not that kind of a van," I explained. "It's a beat-up old yellow van with the windows painted over to hide what is inside."

This time she put the paper down to stare at me. Then she laughed. "Trust Jane to make it sound ominous. It's probably just a handyman that the real estate agent sent to check over the house."

"You think so?" I asked so happily that she looked puzzled.

"What difference does it make anyway?" she asked.

"Oh"—I tried to sound casual—"I thought it was someone who shouldn't be there. Like robbers or something."

"I doubt that," she said calmly, going back to her paper. "Why, Mrs. Cellini's kitchen window must look directly into that house and yard. She'd call the police if anything looked strange."

I started to cut up my French toast and push it around in the hot maple syrup. Then I remembered and got my

51

bands out and hid them under the edge of my plate. I felt better about the van belonging to some workman or other. Then what Mom had said hit me.

Those houses really *are* that close. With the leaves off the hedges, Margaret would be able to see everything that went on at Number Seventeen without even leaving her window. I thought about all the times I had carried food over there to Stilts and how we played in the back yard when I thought no one could see. A funny hard lump got in the way of my French toast.

When I couldn't get my food to go down even with a big drink of milk, I took my plate over to the sink and rinsed it down the garbage disposal before Mom could see how little I had eaten. At the sound of the disposer she made a little leap.

"Heavens," she cried. "I'll be late. Don't forget Dr. Robles and be sure your top button is fastened before you go out."

Then she aimed a kiss at me and shot out the door with the morning paper under her arm along with her purse.

I groaned about the paper. I really needed to read my horoscope. Maybe it could tell me whether the yellow van did belong to a handyman or was an actual omen of doom.

When you start thinking about bad omens, you can sure find a lot of them. I was thinking about Margaret's window when Miss Benson asked me for a metaphor and I gave her a simile instead. All the kids stared because Language is the only place that I don't make mistakes.

When Dr. Robles looked at my bands, he said I would have to be a patient patient because they needed a little more time. Then a black cat ran in front of our bus and I knew something was going to turn out badly with that yellow van.

In one of her magic books, Natalie had had a spell that warded off evil eye. When I tried to think of a spell to help me, that was the only one I could remember. I repeated it all the way home but it didn't help at all. When I turned the corner at Hickory and Barkley, the yellow van was still sitting in the drive as if it belonged there.

Lights were on in Number Seventeen, one at the back where the kitchen is, and one farther up, like the hall, maybe. The blind in Natalie's window was still halfway down the way she left it. We used to signal with our blinds. When Natalie wasn't going to be able to play, she pulled her blind all the way down. If the blind was clear at the top it meant "Come on over." But halfway down was a promise that we would get together later. She had left that blind halfway down when she left the house for the last time.

I had to get food and water to Stilts. And Carson was waggling his tail around and complaining at me for being so late. While I fed Carson I worried about Stilts, which was awfully disloyal. But what if Stilts barked or whined while the person from the yellow van was still in the house?

First water. I couldn't use the outside faucet the way I had been because it made a singing in the house. I rinsed out a vacuum bottle from my lunch box and filled it. With the dog food in the pocket of my jacket, I let myself out the door.

Once I got across the street I crouched down and scampered along the hedge that separates Number Seventeen from Margaret's yard. I didn't see any movement in the houses, but the light from Margaret's kitchen window was yellowish on the hedge.

Lucky for me that Stilts isn't a barker. He just whimpered and pressed hard against the lattice when I squatted down there. I held him tight a few minutes, just loving him and letting him lick my face and dig his head in my neck. Usually when he did that I giggled, but I was extra quiet because of the yellow van. Then I gave him his food and water.

"We can't play," I explained in a whisper, watching him gobble his food in big crackling bites. "Another day we will."

From the house above came a rhythmic sound as if a radio or stereo was on. The light from the breakfast room lay out on the lawn in yellow squares. Then I heard a sudden grating like a door being pushed open and I held my breath.

After the door sound there was only silence for a long time. Then I heard the heavy creaking of weight coming down the steps. I caught Stilts in my arms tight and wriggled way to the back of the hiding place. He wrestled to get back to his food but I held him tight with my hand over his mouth.

The man in the back yard was looking around. Through the cross pieces of the lattice I could see trouser legs with big heavy boots under them. The feet would go a few steps and then the man would stop and listen and then move on again. Finally I heard a gruff voice say, "Your imagination has been running away with you all day, man." Then the trouser legs disappeared, the steps creaked again, and the door shut with a slam.

My clothes were as wet all over as if I had been running. Stilts's heartbeat was always fast but right then it seemed that mine almost matched it. My knees were just nothing, all soft and runny feeling.

The minute I got out of the pen I shot over into Margaret's yard. I sat there a long minute to let my knees get hard again. I could hear kitchen sounds and Margaret singing from inside her house. Then a flash of light played across the yard and I knew Mom's car was turning into our drive on the other side of the street.

I decided this was the world's best time to visit Margaret. As I pressed the doorbell I realized that Margaret would be astonished to see me. What could I say if she asked me why I had stayed away for so long? I tried to remember the last time but I only knew it was before my braces and the braces had already been on forever.

Margaret always turns on the porch light and looks out before she opens the door. She was wearing an apron with tulips sewn on that hung lower than her cut-off pants. A rush of spicy tomato scent spilled out as she swung the door wide.

"Well, if it isn't J.T." She didn't sound particularly surprised, just more pleased than anything. She has always called me J.T. because she had a sister-in-law named Jane who (she said) was a real dog, and she

55

couldn't hang that name on someone she liked. "Come in fast before my sauce burns," she said, turning back toward the kitchen.

I trailed along, trying to think of some excuse for not coming for so long. It turned out that I didn't need to say anything. She stirred the sauce briskly as I watched. Then she fished a bay leaf out of the pan and licked it before throwing it away. After she turned the sauce into a strainer, she wiped her hands on her apron and looked me over carefully.

"That's not a bad job of growing," she said after a minute. Then she leaned forward to stare at my mouth. "What in tarnation is all that?" she asked with interest.

"Braces," I said, showing them to her. "With bands."

She frowned suspiciously. "Are you sure that somebody isn't just taking your folks for a lot of cash?" Margaret is like that. She counts every penny of her change. She even dickers with the man who brings produce around in a truck, and he already has his prices written on a sign with crayon. "It's not the money," she explained to me once. "I just can't abide being made a fool of."

"Dr. Robles is supposed to be a very good orthodontist," I reassured her. "And honest, too."

"Your teeth didn't used to be crooked," she said accusingly as if I had gone out and bent them myself.

"My teeth are still okay," I told her. "I had a crossbite." Then I started getting red like I do whenever I think of that word. Natalie was really excited when I got my braces and I had to draw her a picture and everything to show why I needed to have braces because I chewed funny. She frowned at my sketches and said, "Oh, I see. You have this pointy little upper jaw and then a bottom one like a mule shoe."

The very next time I saw Dr. Robles I learned that the right word was crossbite. Crossbite may sound like a mean dog but it's better than the way she said it.

Margaret thought about the word and grinned. "Well, if your folks can afford it and it doesn't spoil the real pleasures of life . . . like gumdrop cookies."

I giggled because ever since I was little Margaret always made gumdrop cookies for us to eat while we played games at her kitchen table.

Margaret glanced at her clock. "That sauce needs to drip for a half hour. Want to play something?"

When I called Mom she said it was okay for just a half hour because it was Dad's night to come in from a trip and he would be like a bear.

While Margaret set the timer she asked, "What do you like to play now that you are so old that you have to have your teeth braced up?"

I had forgotten what games she had.

"Can you play Dominoes?" she asked after a minute. "Not just fitting them together but really playing with a scorecard and points and everything?"

When I looked doubtful, she said briskly, "High time."

After I got the hang of it, the game was fun. She got a gas bill envelope out of her "total mess" drawer and kept our scores on it. I had five points and she had fifteen when the whole house shook with the sound of grinding gears and the roar of a motor.

She paused with a tile in her hand and said, "That will be Mr. Garvic next door. The van moved him in today."

"The yellow van?" I asked.

"Oh my, no," she said. "A big moving van. That yellow thing is just what he drives instead of a car."

I couldn't see anything to make a point so I just laid down my double three on the end.

"He ought to be a nice neighbor," she said contentedly. "He is really crazy about that house. He never had anything but an apartment before and he's already talking about making a garden come spring. He's young like your folks. We had a good talk when he came over to borrow my phone."

The timer started dinging that the half hour was up.

I put the tiles back in their box while she hung up our scorecard by her wall phone. "When you get over again we'll play that game out. Like a tournament."

While I was getting my jacket on she mentioned the man next door again. "I imagine he's a pretty nice-looking fellow under all that hair and that beard."

I ran across the street with Margaret watching from her porch as she had when I was little.

Mom had taken the roast out and was making gravy. She had put on fresh lipstick and the smell of her perfume was mixed with the brown smell of the roast. That reminded me that Dad was due any time.

"Good timing." Mom smiled at me over her shoulder. "Use the green napkins tonight."

58

I was going to tell her about Mr. Garvic moving in across the street but we heard Dad's car and both ran to meet him. When neither of them mentioned the lights in Number Seventeen I didn't either. I wanted to keep from thinking about it at all, wondering what would happen if Stilts whined or barked and that man with the heavy boots and the beard and all found him.

7

"Storms and Screams"

Saturdays are always special at our house because they are project days. Since Mom and Dad both work and I go to school (which Dad says is the same as having a job), we all pitch in and run the house together. Of course Saturdays is the only day we have to do the big jobs.

Once when she wanted to play and I couldn't, Natalie said that Dad ran our house like Nazi Germany. Later I made her take it back, but she never did understand how great it is the way we work together, the three of us.

Big projects are always written on the bulletin board in slogans that my dad makes up. "Once a salesman, always a salesman," my mom says. In early fall there is "Up, Up and Away" for the day we rake leaves, pack them into bags and haul them off. "Spit and Polish" means cleaning out the basement and garage. (The spit part is for the fighting we do with Mom before she lets Dad and me keep stuff that we think will come in handy later but she thinks is junk.)

"Storms and Screams" is the last big job of fall. That is the day we take down screens and hang the storm windows for winter. That screams is a joke on me because I used to say "scream door" when I was little and still got words wrong.

The day after Mr. Garvic moved into Number Seventeen was Storm and Scream Saturday. We drew straws for the jobs the way we always do. I hate to accuse my own father of cheating but it is mighty mysterious the way he always gets the straw for going up and down the ladder. He gets to hang things while Mom and I wash windows with a big sponge that leaks stinky stuff up our sleeves and freezes our elbows.

While I made trips in and out of the garage with the screens, I kept an eye on Number Seventeen. After Margaret told me that Mr. Garvic had really moved in, I knew I had to move Stilts away from there. I didn't have any place figured out, but I thought I could tie him behind our garage just for the weekend until I figured something else out. Anything was better than having him discovered by that strange man.

Right after breakfast the yellow van drove away. It would have been a perfect chance for me to slip over and get Stilts if Mom and Dad had not both been out working with me. In just a little while I was glad I hadn't tried because the yellow van was back in the drive again.

The other fun thing about big-project Saturdays is that we always get to go out to dinner that night. Sometimes we go for barbecue and sometimes pizza, but we all like to eat Chinese the best.

The yellow van came and went all day, just driving me crazy. We were finished with our work and cleaned up way before dinner and I still hadn't had a chance to go get Stilts. Dad settled down to do reports at his desk and Mom started going through all the magazines she had gotten behind on.

Having the storm windows up made the house very quiet. I could hear the occasional screech of Dad's pen and the rustle of Mom's pages. Carson's purr was a comfortable rumble from across the room. Everyone was peaceful but me. Finally I decided to go over to Margaret's. I wouldn't be able to get Stilts, maybe, but at least I would be closer to him.

I saw that kids were playing at the top of the hill but I didn't stare. I did realize that they got quiet when I crossed the street. There was some extra kid with Gerry and Steve Jarvis and I could just feel them all stopping to say something ugly to him about me.

Margaret had a scarf tied around her head and was chopping nuts on a wooden board. A bowl of shiny cubed fruit was at her side.

"Christmas fruitcake," she explained, waving her big knife at the stuff spread all around.

"It's not even Thanksgiving yet," I pointed out.

She shrugged and set a plate over the glistening fruit. "The longer it soaks the better it is. That's what they say. I never could stand the stuff myself. I just don't hold with eating food that bites back."

I giggled because there is something in fruitcake that

snaps on my tongue, too. "Then why do you make it?" I asked.

She kind of laughed. "It's one of the ruts I have gotten into in my old age, J.T." Her voice was confidential. "My nephews rave about it so I keep on making it. For all I know they could hate the stuff but don't dare tell me after all this time. And it gives me something festive to do."

"Don't stop for me," I said when I realized she was putting her stuff away.

"I can chop nuts any old time," she replied airily. "We have a tournament to run here. And I made fresh cookies just in case you came today."

Mom thinks that Margaret talks a lot because she is lonely. I think she just likes to talk. Sometimes she even talks to herself while she works and to the plants that hang in her windows. She started to chatter as soon as we got the dominoes out.

"Have you met the new boy yet?" she asked.

"New boy?" I asked.

"Duke Garvic," she said, making a ten-point start with her first tile. "The boy next door."

"Next door," I repeated dumbly. "At Number Seventeen?" I realized I sounded stupid but I really couldn't believe what she was saying.

"That's right," she agreed. "The Lowery house. He and his mom live off somewhere but he gets to spend weekends with his dad. Maybe not every weekend," she revised after a minute. "I don't really understand that custody business too well. But I do know that Mr. Garvic changed his job and rented this house just to

63

have a good place for Duke to come home to on weekends."

It never bothers Margaret that I don't talk much because she is used to me. She just chatters on without waiting.

"I guess there's a funny custody thing with them anyway. Duke and his mom don't get along. Duke says his mom loves him okay but doesn't really like him. That's why he wants to live with his dad."

"Then why doesn't he just move in with his dad and stay?" I asked. The whole thing sounded silly and involved to me.

Margaret laughed and made another scoring move. "That's exactly what I asked and then I wished I hadn't. Duke says his mom feels really guilty about her feelings and won't admit them even to herself. The court gave the custody to her but if she would just face her feelings and let Duke go, they would all be happier."

I shook my head. I hate thinking about things like that. All kids wonder what they would do if their parents quit wanting to be married any more. But that was somebody else's problem. My problem was to get Stilts out of that hiding place fast. The boy, whatever Margaret had called him, would find Stilts right off the first time he had a good look around the yard.

Then I remembered the extra boy at the top of the hill with Gerry and Steve Jarvis. "Maybe I saw him out playing with the kids," I said.

She nodded. "Like as not. He's a friendly, talkative sort of kid. Warm."

A little whirl of scared excitement started in me. I

had been waiting for the yellow van to leave but that might take a day or two. I needed to get Stilts out that minute and I would have a better chance of getting it done with a grownup in the house than a boy. I had to go get Stilts while the boy was still up there with the Jarvis kids. I had his leash in my pocket but no food. If I even had a cookie, maybe I could keep him quiet in my arms while I got him away from that house. I could worry about where to fasten him behind our garage after I got him away safe.

I took another cookie from the plate and nibbled at it. "These sure are good," I told Margaret, waiting for a chance to put the rest of it into my pocket.

"Finish them off if you want to," she said. "That recipe makes for an army."

"I'd better stop now," I said with the cookie safely tucked away. "In fact I probably ought to go home and get dressed. We are going out to eat Chinese tonight."

I listened outside Margaret's door. I could still hear the shouts of boys up the street. I walked along the hedge where I could see the glow of light from Number Seventeen. When I was just even with the end of the house I darted through the hedge really fast and started toward the hiding place under the breakfast room.

I was fishing the cookie out of my pocket before I realized that someone had followed me around the house and was standing there watching me. Then the voice came, angry and short.

"What do you think you are doing?"

My instinct was to run but the boy who was standing close to me was so much bigger than I that I just stared

65

at him. He looked about my age, maybe a small twelve or a big eleven. He wasn't exactly fat but he had that square, strong look that boys sometimes have. His hair was cottony light and he had on a full set of railroad tracks just like mine only I couldn't see any bands.

"Well!" he said, to remind me that he was waiting.

When I am scared I try to make myself sound like Natalie because she always handled things so well.

"I was on my way home," I said in that insulted-sounding voice Natalie often used when she wanted to get rid of somebody.

Then he frowned a little and said "Hey, I know who you are. You're the stuck-up snob from across the street."

"I am no such thing," I protested, feeling my face redden.

"Then what are you doing here?" he challenged.

"You don't own this house," I said. "Natalie does and I am Natalie's best friend."

"Some kind of answer," he sneered. "I've already heard about the two of you. You have every right to be Natalie Lowery's slave if you want to be but you don't have to be a dirty spy, too."

His voice rose strangely. I got the sudden feeling that in spite of his loud words he was afraid of something. "Go on," he ordered roughly. "You just go on and get out of this yard. And stay out! We don't need any spies around here carrying tales."

I stared at him as I backed toward the street. He was afraid of me. That made no sense at all. He was bigger

66

and stronger and it really was his house and yet he was afraid of me. Why?

I was already at the curb and still he was shouting after me.

"Don't you forget that you are right here and she is a long way away. If you make trouble I can get even with you. I'll make you sorry if you make trouble, and don't think I won't."

At first I had wanted to get away fast for fear Stilts might hear our voices and start to whine. Now I wanted away because he was so mean and threatening when I hadn't done a thing except stand in his yard.

Dad had left his desk to watch TV and Mom was in the shower when I let myself in and slipped back to my room. Carson woke from his warm place on the bed and came to rub his flat tall hips against me, purring. I hugged him close to help me get rid of that scared feeling that Duke Garvic had given me. Then, just like the bolt of lightning illuminating the porch, I realized why Duke Garvic was afraid of me.

The Lowerys had said their house could not be rented to anyone with children or pets. Now that Mr. Lowery had brought Duke in there he had broken the rules. Since the Jarvis boys had obviously told him that Natalie and I were best friends, he had to be afraid that I would tattle on him and his dad to Natalie and get them kicked out of the house.

I would never have thought of it in a million years but now that he had put the idea in my head I sat stunned.

If Natalie's dad kicked them out I would have the

hiding place for Stilts as long as I needed it. All I had to do was get my dog away until Natalie told her dad the news and out they would go. But it was winter, only two weeks from Thanksgiving. I had to hurry.

I was upset even while I was writing the letter. I had never done anything that mean before, even if I was doing it for a good reason like saving Stilts. It was Natalie herself who had showed me how to tell something without really lying but certainly not telling the truth. You just pick out what to say and what to leave out at the same time. I even selected words that I knew had some extra meaning for Natalie.

I told her that the new people were not our kind. I said that the father was bearded and wore big boots and drove a battered yellow van like the hippies do. I told her how his rude ugly son had said terrible things about her even though he had never even seen her.

On the way to the restaurant Dad handed me a bunch of his reports to stick into the post office slot. I tucked my letter to Natalie in among the others and mailed it off airmail.

When we eat Chinese everyone orders one thing and then Dad adds something extra. Mom ordered the hot and sour soup and I asked for those little fried wontons that they call pot stickers. Then Dad picked out sweet and sour pork and those crunchy flat pea pods. I like all those things really well but somehow nothing tasted as good as it usually did.

When Dad asked why I wasn't eating, Mom reminded him that I had been to the orthodontist the day before and he nodded.

Dad opened his fortune cookie first and read it aloud. I opened mine too, but after I read it I hid it in my hand and took another one really quick.

"What is your fate?" Dad asked as he warmed up my cup of oolong tea.

I read the second fortune to them. "Do not throw away the oyster of life while searching for the pearl."

"Classic," Dad said, counting out money on the tray for the waitress.

I read the first fortune I had gotten over again when I got back home. It sounded as ominous as it had the first time. The only possible thing that fortune could refer to was the letter I had just mailed to Natalie. After all, as Duke Garvic himself had said, she was a long way away and he was close. I pressed the creases out of the fortune to read it a third time and just wanted to die.

I had only written the mean letter to save Stilts who was hungry and needing water over there under Number Seventeen. The cookie had not held a fortune at all but a warning to me: "He who gambles must be prepared to lose all."

8

Behind the Lattice

It turned really cold during the night after we got our storm windows up. "Talk about timing," Dad said when he came in to waken me the next morning. Off in the basement I could hear the furnace blowing, but still the air in my room was cold.

"Frost stars," Dad said, touching the heavy tracery of ice that had formed inside my window. Then he sighed. "Well, it has to come before it can go."

"Don't you like winter?" I asked, watching the feathery lace melt away from the warmth of his fingertip.

"Sure I like it." He took my hand and folded my fingers over and grinned in that mischievous way he does. "Everybody likes to have thermal underwear twisting around under their clothes, and cars that won't start in the morning, and bright blue toes from frostbite." Then he grinned again. "Maybe I just worry about my girls' being cold and uncomfortable."

"We do fine," I told him. But how was Stilts doing? I hadn't been able to take him food and water since Friday and it was Sunday.

When I sat up in bed a blast of cold air tunneled down the back of my nightie. In that place under the porch it must be freezing. He had nothing to burrow under there in his pen, not even a pile of old leaves to keep him warm.

But it was the water that worried me the most. Dogs and people can go without food for quite a while but he would die without water. Would he know enough to lick the frozen pan of water and melt it on his tongue?

Seeing me shiver, Dad pulled my housecoat from the hook on the closet door and wrapped it around me with a hug. "Go polish your artillery so we can have pancakes with hot maple syrup."

I didn't feel very much like making jokes, but I hate to let Dad down. Artillery indeed. I tried to make up something funny about people with artillery on their teeth shooting off at the mouth, but by the time I had it worked out he was off in the kitchen with Mom, laughing about something else.

I put Carson in the warm place I had left and wished I had taken a woolly blanket for Stilts instead of those old cold towels. But surely Duke would go back to his mother today. Then I could feed Stilts and water him and put him somewhere safe and comfortable.

The day warmed slowly. I couldn't think of anything but Stilts and the way he must feel. By noon the frost stars were all gone from the window and the line in the thermometer was rising. The wind blew briskly and the

71

Jarvis boys brought out a new silver kite like the one that got ruined. Gerry managed to get it way up above Barkley Street where it hung like a glistening banner.

Dad challenged Mom and me to a few games of Hearts by the fire. I drew eight clubs in my first hand and tricked them both. By the time they realized what was happening I had the lead in clubs, and as Dad said, I beat them "hearts down." From my chair I could see the stretch of street in front of Number Seventeen and most of Margaret's front yard. Gerry and Steve Jarvis had come down with the kite and Duke Garvic was out there with them. Pretty soon Tracy pulled Mugs up in his wagon to watch. You could only see the line of Mugs's eyes between his stocking cap and his muffler.

It was really strange to see Barkley Street like that with all the kids playing together. I glanced over to see if Dad had noticed. If he did, he was sure to grin and talk about his dream of a "Barkley Street Six-pack." But his chair was at a bad angle to see out of doors so I just watched them myself, feeling strangely lonely even though I was right there between my own mom and dad.

Mugs was struggling to get out of the wagon. Then I saw Duke hand him the kite string. Mugs gripped it with both mittens as Steve started to run and pull the wagon behind him. The kite pitched and dived and disappeared into Margaret's back yard. Gerry ran off like a shot to retrieve it.

When I chuckled, Dad got up and looked out. "Who's the big tall boy?" he asked.

"He's from Number Seventeen," I said, watching

Gerry try to untangle the string from Margaret's snow-ball bush.

"But I thought the Lowerys had forbidden children and pets," Mom said, sounding surprised. Then she glanced at Dad and didn't say any more.

"Can you love someone without liking them?" I asked, thinking what Margaret had said about Duke and his mother.

Dad laughed the way he always does when I change the subject of the conversation without any warning.

But Mom answered right off. "That's silly. How could you love someone you don't like?"

Dad's eyes sparkled the way they do when he teases. "Let's take the case of your Aunt Flo," he suggested mildly.

Mom didn't think that was funny. She shuffled the deck in a swift rush of color. "That's different," she said finally, snapping the cards into piles.

I picked up my cards fast so she wouldn't see that I was grinning, too.

Aunt Flo is my grandmother's sister. When my grandmother died, Mom felt sorry for Aunt Flo and invited her and her family for Thanksgiving dinner. That was way before I was born, and they still come every year whether Mom invites them or not. Aunt Flo makes my mom nervous. Mom whips around cleaning and cooking and frowning for weeks before they come. Then she hardly opens her mouth while Aunt Flo and her family are here. She just keeps smiling all the time with one of those pasted-on looking smiles that clowns have.

73

But Aunt Flo doesn't know the difference. She just talks and complains and tells us how much better everything used to be in the old days and looks into the corners with the edges of her eyes.

Finally Mom grinned too and said, "Touché."

Dad says that is French for, "You win this time, Buster, but you better watch your step from now on."

After the hearts game was over I nearly went wild with worry. I just knew that Stilts was suffering and that stupid Duke Garvic didn't have sense enough to go away somewhere else. I got the thermos filled and the dog food all ready in my pocket while Dad was napping and Mom was in the kitchen starting dinner and making pumpkin pies.

Finally I saw Duke come out of the house with a satchel in his hand. He stood by the yellow van a long time talking to his dad. He didn't look as tall as he had out in the back yard or when he was playing with the other kids. He looked bent over and not very happy as they stood there and talked together.

Then I saw Mr. Garvic touch him on the shoulder the way my dad does me. Duke threw the satchel into the van and they drove off.

The minute the van had turned the corner, I started across the street as casually as I could, trying to make it look as if I were going to Margaret's.

The wind had died down and the sky was that flat color like pewter. The grass along the hedges crinkled under my feet with cold.

At the back of the house I kneeled down because right off I could see there was something strange about the lattice. The panels that were supposed to be on the inside of the supports had been pulled to the outside. One was loose and banging softly as I squatted down to look.

"Stilts," I called, really afraid. With the panel on the outside, all he had to do to get out was just to press against the lattice and it would give.

I kept calling but there was only the rustle of leaves and that soft banging of the panel. A car went by in the street in front and I waited until it was past. Then I crawled inside. Everything was there—the water dish with a little solid ice in the bottom, the empty kibble plate, and the bath towels scrunched up the way they looked after Stilts played with them. But Stilts was gone.

It was icy cold in there. The ground was rough and uneven under my jeans. Even as I crawled all the way around, telling myself that he might be hiding, I knew in my heart that he had wandered off into that wintry night.

I finally gave up and sat on the icy ground, letting myself get colder and colder to punish myself. Maybe I would freeze. After a long long time someone would find me there. They would all say I had died of exposure because grownups never think that a kid could die of a broken heart.

A hard tinny sound like a car door slamming brought me to my senses. I could already hear footsteps in the house above me as I dumped the new kibble into the plate and poured in the water just in case. Then I crept home along Margaret's hedge, pressing my hands against my eyes to take away the look of crying.

Dad glanced up at me as I passed through the living room. "Tears, Janie?" he asked with sudden concern.

I blinked at him and made myself laugh. "Very icy wind," I explained.

"Well do I know." He stretched and handed me the handkerchief from his back pocket. Then he pulled me down in the big chair to watch the weather forecast. "Look at that," he said with surprise. "They are already predicting snow."

I don't even remember eating dinner but I must have. I must have made it through the rest of the evening without acting as strange as I felt inside because finally I was in my room alone. I slumped down on my bed feeling helpless and hopeless and sick inside my heart.

I hadn't even thought very much about Natalie in the weeks since Stilts came. I had thought about magic even less, but all of a sudden I wanted to believe in magic like everything.

Natalie'd had some black powder that she poured into a dish and said some strange words over. Then she had pricked my finger and dropped three drops of blood into the powder. When the blood got dry it was all black and she wrapped the whole mess in a piece of cloth and buried it. The wart on my left thumb and the two in my right palm were supposed to wither away as the black powder and blood withered away in the ground.

It worked. It took a long time but about three months later the warts got smaller and flatter and went away just as she said they would.

Then there was a boy named Leonard who started in our school about halfway through. He wasn't like any boy I had ever known before. He looked at me all the time. I hated it because even when I didn't look around I could feel his eyes on the back of my head. Every time he got near me he hit me on the shoulder or arm or wherever he could reach me. I tried to stay out of his way and I tried to dodge when that fist came shooting out at me, but nothing did any good until Natalie used a spell on him.

She took a lot of strange things and wouldn't even tell me where she got them, and she made a little fire in a pie plate in her back yard. Her mother came out screaming at the first wisp of smoke, but the stuff flared up with a bad smell and Natalie said the spell had burned long enough to make it work.

And it did. Within a week or two Leonard quit paying any attention to me at all. He didn't quit acting funny, but instead of me he started staring all the time at Kimberley Johnson, and she had little blue bruises on her arm from his hitting her before school was out.

I wished I were Natalie. If I were Natalie I could do some charm or say some spell and know where Stilts was and go get him and bring him home.

But I was not Natalie, and the whole line of magic books in my closet were just so much paper and cardboard to me. Natalie gave them to me as presents and swore that I could do anything if I just learned enough. The only time I could even make a wish come true was when I was careful to wish for something I knew would happen anyway.

77

Mom said that all of magic was bunk. I was beginning to think she was right. How could you make someone love you or ward off doom by whispering some silly thing over and over to yourself? Maybe the warts would have gone away by themselves in that same three months. Maybe Leonard would have changed his mind about who he wanted to stare at and hit in that same week or two. Magic was an okay game to play for a good shivery feeling about something that didn't matter. But Stilts mattered, Stilts was real. He was hungry and thirsty and shivering somewhere in the cold, and magic was worse than nothing. It was false, like a promise made with your fingers crossed.

I couldn't kid myself about magic and I couldn't help Stilts by throwing myself down for a good cry. I had to do something sensible.

The word "sensible" always reminds me of Miss Benson. She gave us some arithmetic problems that you couldn't just add or subtract or divide. "You have to use your heads on these," she had said brightly. "Solve the problem as you would a real problem in your life. Make a list of possible things you could do and write them down. Check each idea and eliminate the ones that won't work. In time you will find a way to solve the problem."

So I wrote down possible ways to find Stilts.

Number One: Run an ad in the newspaper advertising for him.

Checking it: The only phone number I could list would be our phone at home. Mom and Dad would find out what I had done to that poor puppy. Anyway I didn't have enough money to pay for the ad, much less the reward which is always offered.

Number Two: Put up a sign in the grocery store and at the city hall and all over like people do with bake sales.

Checking it: Again, there was only our own phone to write on the notice and, even if someone did find Stilts and call Mom and Dad, he would have to go to the pound and be put to sleep in three days.

Number Three: Call the animal refuge place myself and make my voice sound old and tell them that his collar got torn off and to call me when he was brought in.

Checking it: They charge fifteen dollars to get back a dog that is brought in. I had two quarters and a handful of pennies to last until December.

Miss Benson was wrong. There isn't always a way to solve a problem. I crawled into bed with Carson and curled around him, hurting inside.

When Dad came to tuck me in, I pretended to be asleep. He stood there in the dark a long while with his hand lying very softly on my head, funny tufty hair and all. He stared out at the fine spinning flakes that were beginning to blow along Barkley Street. His hand felt a lot warmer than the 98.6 degrees that people are supposed to be.

And there was more to his touch than warmth. It was as if the strength of his caring filled the air around the two of us. If I hadn't given up magic, I would probably have claimed that sense as magic. What Dad brought into the room with him was real and you could feel the pain in it.

Loving hurts.

I realized with a kind of shock that when I miss Natalie, a lot of it is just that I am alone and miss having her there to entertain me. This kind of loving, like Dad and Mom and I have, and what I feel for Carson and Stilts, has a kind of pain lying under the joy of it.

I cried even harder after Dad closed my door and went away.

9

Coconut Macaroons

At my last school conference, Miss Benson told Mom that I was in the top third percentile in vocabulary. I know Dad was pleased because he teased me about it all the time. I like words and I thought I really knew the meanings of a lot of them until Stilts disappeared. But there is a great deal of difference between being able to define a word on a test and really knowing what it meant.

Take the words *bleak, dismal,* and *despair.*

Bleak means going out on your bike every night after school, wheeling up and down strange streets, watching and listening and only seeing and hearing the wrong things.

Dismal is an emptiness in your chest when you hear the wind howl and imagine a tufty little dog cringing in an alley somewhere, cold and hungry and crying down deep in his throat the way he did when he wanted me to stay and play some more and I had to leave him.

And *despair* means just what the dictionary says: without hope. But that doesn't explain what happens inside you when hope has gone.

You have the same outside shape and your voice sounds the same, but inside you are empty. A hollowness is in everything. Ginger cookies might as well be mashed turnips for the way they taste. People can say the very nicest things to you and you nod and say, "Yeah, sure." The only thing that wells up from that hollowness is tears, and they come without warning. A dog howling off somewhere will flood your eyes in the middle of a class. Even nice things like having Carson butting his head against you to wake you up will bring a sudden sobbing, because Carson is warm and happy and purring and Stilts is out there somewhere in the cold blackness alone.

School went on that week as usual. We finished our unit in electricity and all the boys got A's and I was lucky to pass for all I cared about it. We finished the Incas and started in on Canada. But all the time, even with hope gone, I had to keep searching for Stilts. Love isn't something that stops when it gets useless. I told myself that the very act of my looking might make him safer wherever he was.

Margaret and I kept on with our domino tournament when I got home from my nightly search for Stilts. I found out that Margaret had started a domino tournament with Duke Garvic too, but I was too numb even to care.

Mom spent every evening making pies and cinnamon rolls and cookies for the freezer. Thanksgiving was only a week away and there was never enough of anything when Aunt Flo came with her family.

The snow came on Friday. They said it was a record breaker for so early in the season. It was a silent snow. Not that most snows are really noisy, but this one was spooky quiet, starting in the night without so much as a breath of wind. I wakened to it for no reason. The sky was as pale as if it were morning, but the light seemed to come from the snow which was piled everywhere, on every tiniest twig. The sides of the trees were pillared with it. It was a white hush laid on the world. Even the city snowplow, flashing along the street with its amber light eerie against my window, made hardly any sound.

I cleaned the walks off before school because Dad has some strange terror of being sued for icy walks. The cars snarled by as I worked, their power trapped in that softness. By the time I got home from school that afternoon there were only extra shadowy mounds where I had thrown the snow back and the walks were filled up again.

I could only think of how high that snow would come on Stilts's legs. I could see him stumbling in it, weak and unsure of himself. The only thing I wanted in the whole wide world was for Stilts to be safe somewhere, warm and loved. Because I cried without meaning to that whole week, my nose began to run all the time.

Mom poked stuff at me and fumed. ''I swear you are going to have that nasty runny cold all winter.'' I just let her think it really was a cold.

Duke got there that Saturday in spite of the snowstorm. He barely got his satchel inside the house before he had the Jarvis boys out helping him shovel Margaret's walks. They built a fort by the hedge that separates the houses and had snowball wars. They left their boots on Margaret's porch in an untidy line and trooped in for cookies, and probably cocoa which she makes with plenty of vanilla and a blob of thick cream on top.

I felt left out and sad and I tried to think of every ugly thing Natalie had said about those kids, but somehow things Natalie said sounded strange when you thought about them later. They only sounded convincing when she was right there with those dark eyes on you so alive and powerful.

By the time Duke left on Sunday afternoon I felt as if I had been forever inside with just Mom and Dad and Carson. I was heartsick about Stilts and prickly with jealousy when I went over to visit Margaret.

I almost didn't ring the bell when I got to the porch. The house was really noisy and someone in there was shouting. Then I remembered that when Margaret watches football on TV she yells a lot and tells the players what a bad job they are doing.

Margaret had on slacks that came all the way down and over them an artist's smock with a pallette on the pocket. She grinned at me and backed toward the TV set.

"You don't have to quit watching for me," I told her in a shout because the volume was so high.

She waved a dismissing hand. "Never turn down a live friend for a dead flash of light," she shouted back, her voice suddenly too loud for the room when the TV stopped. "Where have you been all weekend?"

"Oh, at home," I said, not looking up for fear she would have that sharp searching glance on my face. I hoped she wouldn't ask why I wasn't out there with the other kids. I knew Dad had thought about it and purposely not asked.

She didn't either. She just set out the dominoes and the scorecard. "Your mom and dad all right?" she asked.

I nodded, turning the bone pile over.

There was something different between us. It was as if she was trying to find things to talk to me about. We'd never had that trouble before.

"I guess you hear all the time from your friend Natalie?" she asked, studying her draw of tiles.

"Once in a while," I told her. It seemed disloyal to mention that Natalie was not the best letter writer ever. "She's awfully busy in that new place."

Margaret looked up but she didn't seem to be seeing me. Instead she stared past me through the window to the bleached winter sky beyond. "It's always harder for the one who stays behind," she said.

For no reason at all I remembered how it was before Mr. Cellini died, how they used to walk together in the evening. They would go off toward the park and come back a long time later, walking the same slow way with their heads bent together in talk.

After a minute she jumped up and said, "I even forgot to offer you a cookie, J.T. I made fresh ones today too, seeing as how I ran completely out yesterday."

She gave a quirky smile as if it was fun to be reminded of what a good time she had had with Duke and the others.

I stared at the cookies on the saucer. Margaret makes a lot of different kinds, the gumdrop ones that we both like, oatmeal with currants in, and a rolled butterscotch that has gummy date stuff in between. These were different. They were a pale tan color with hairy coconut sticking out and a red sugary blob right in the middle of every one. I could never stand the taste of coconut in my whole life, and since I have braces I just knew those little strings would grab onto my wires and hang on until thunder.

"Coconut macaroons," she explained. "Duke likes them the best of all, even if they are hard for him to eat with his braces. With candied cherries," she added, as if I couldn't see those awful red eyes staring back at me.

I didn't remind Margaret that I didn't like coconut. I just said they were beautiful but it was probably too close to dinner for me to eat sweets. She looked at me sort of funny because that has never stopped me before.

Usually I go home from Margaret's feeling better than I did when I went. That day was different. I didn't feel jealous any more but I felt tired and kind of sick. Everything in my whole life was going away from me. First I lost Natalie, and then Stilts, and now Margaret was moving away from me toward Duke in her feelings. I couldn't even stand to think of that letter I had written Natalie trying to get her to have her folks take the house away from Mr. Garvic. What would happen when Mr. Lowery made Duke and his dad leave Barkley Street because of me? There wouldn't be a single soul on the whole street who could stand me, including myself. And it wouldn't help anybody now that Stilts was gone.

I was barely inside the house before Dad called to me from his desk. "Hey, Jane, I have an apology. You had a letter mixed up with the Saturday mail that I didn't look at. I only found it here after you left." He handed me that square red envelope that Natalie always uses, and grinned. "You are just lucky I ever found it in that pile of bills."

I almost burst with happiness. Here I was in the dumps and I got a letter. I pushed Carson off the warm place to curl up and read it. It was two whole pages. Even when someone writes big like Natalie does, it still takes a while to read two whole pages.

I only read the letter once. The words stuck to my mind like snow to frozen mittens. I couldn't make them go away no matter how hard I tried.

Dear, dear Jane,

Have I ever got stupendous news! I told you how lousy the kids are here, remember? Well, it's better now. I met a new girl whose dad was transferred in from Indiana and her name is Carolyn Ann. She's not like me at all—in fact she's what I call colorless. She really needs someone to help her make it. She's shy and not pretty and scared of everything. I have taken her under my wing just

87

like I did you and she is really learning fast just like you did.

I told her I would be her best friend and I'd take care of her. But don't worry though. I never told her that she would be *my* best friend.

I crossed my fingers anyway so nothing is changed between us.

I wish you would tell me what came of your premonition. I get a lot of psychic waves here but mostly it is just kids being hateful or letting me know how jealous they are.

There was a lot more but it was the same old Natalie stuff. I sat there in shock. Natalie had a new best friend. Crossing your fingers doesn't mean anything. If you say "best friend" right out like that, then you are a best friend and that's all there is to it.

Natalie came back to me suddenly in that really live way that she used to before I found Stilts and started being friendly with Margaret again. I saw her as plainly as if she were right there in my room.

I saw her leaning toward me with her eyes so bright and eager the way they always were. I could even smell her bubble bath and see the dress she had worn that first day, how crisp the pleats had been and how the collar was pointed with a jagged line of handwork joining it to an extra little strip.

What had she said to me that day? What had she actually said in words? Had she said that we would be best friends forever and ever, the way I had always remembered it?

88

No, she hadn't.

She had said that she would be my best friend forever and ever. She didn't ever say that I would be her best friend. That had been one of those tricks with words that she was so proud of, a trick where you say something to make it sound as if you had said something else.

She had promised me nothing. She had only said that I would have her for a best friend forever and she was still free to cross her fingers and take people over like she had me and this new Carolyn Ann.

I could even see a letter she might have written someone about me. How I had rat-colored hair, all tufty, and jaws that didn't match. A namby-pamby because I let my parents push me around. How she would take care of me, teach me.

The room was cool but I flushed hot as the memories clapped by like slides in a projector being cast full size and shameless against my understanding. I wanted to shout at Natalie across the rest of the country and the ocean and everything else that lay between me and Germany.

You did too spoil Gerry's kite on purpose!

You did too take his skate because magic can't carry a skate and hide it like that!

You never did write me a single postcard from that resort in Canada and then you made me feel bad because I didn't get any!

Where had my head been all that time? Why, I'd actually had a premonition of my own the minute I met Natalie. I hadn't liked her. I had been afraid of her, and I had been right. The magic she used on me was leading me to believe lies about myself—"mysterious," and words like that. I had stared at myself in a silly fake hairpiece and seen a Jane Todd I never saw before and decided to be her instead of myself. Dumb. Dumb. Dumb.

It didn't make it any better that a lot of other people had been fooled too. Everybody had made such a big fuss over her at school because she was so vivid and pretty and had been in so many places and made them feel so important with those eager smiles. I had wanted to feel important too, so I lied to myself. Natalie hadn't told me that many lies. She just asked questions and let me answer them out of my own dumbness. "You don't think I ruined that kite on purpose, do you, Jane?" she had asked. "You don't think I stole that skate, do you?" she had asked. "Why would anyone steal just one skate?"

I might have cried or exploded all over the walls of my room if Mom and Dad had not burst in grinning like two big kids. "Wait until you hear," Dad was chortling. "Hey, Jane, just wait until you hear."

Mom was breaking up to keep from giggling as Dad went on. "Thanksgiving," he explained. "We get to have Thanksgiving without Aunt Flo and her troops."

I stared at him. I couldn't remember Thanksgiving any other way. I had never slept in my own room on that holiday or had a turkey wishbone for my own. I had never even liked to draw Pilgrims and Indians because of that boring awful holiday.

"What happened to them?" I asked, having this sudden wonderful vision of a giant tornado picking them

90

all up like Dorothy and Toto and taking them a lot farther with no coming back.

"Your uncle Eddie, Aunt Flo's oldest son, bought a place in Florida and invited them all down there," Mom replied with a giggle. "What will I do with all those pies and rolls I have baked?"

"You mean I can eat at the table with you two?" It was just too big to understand all at once.

Dad broke in. "I've got it. We'll choose our own company this year. How about Jane's friend, Mrs. Cellini? She puts up with this monster all the time. Surely she can stand us for one meal. Imagine, getting to pick your own guests for Thanksgiving!"

I shoved the pain of Natalie's letter clear to the bottom of my mind. Margaret for Thanksgiving. I was almost too excited to talk. "She loves football, Dad," I told him all in a rush. "And she yells at it just like you do. Can I ask her myself?"

"Pick up the phone," Dad suggested.

"Oh, no." I shook my head. "I want to ask her face-to-face." I ran to the window but Margaret's lights were out except the one at the back that she leaves on when she goes to bed. That was all right. I could do it the very next day after school.

Margaret for Thanksgiving. I couldn't believe it.

That evening I stayed in the living room with Mom and Dad, sitting on Dad's lap a long time until they sent me away because the next day was a school day.

I clung to Margaret in my mind desperately. Stilts had been gone exactly a week and the furious shame of

91

my understanding of Natalie was like a sore place inside me. Margaret was my only warm friend outside of Mom and Dad and Carson. And she was going to have Thanksgiving with us. I had to believe it.

10

Margaret's Window

Margaret was gone when I got home from school. I rang the bell several times and even knocked on the door, but the house had that listening feeling that comes when nobody is inside.

I took Carson and a stack of cream cheese-and-jelly sandwiches on crackers up on my bed so I could watch for her to come home. Carson fought me for the cheese on the crackers so I ate them up fast after sharing around the edges where there wasn't any jelly. I did my homework and had a few pages read in my library book before I saw a cab coming up Barkley Street.

After the cab driver set a whole lot of paper sacks on Margaret's porch, she counted money into his hand. By that time I had my wraps on and was picking up the first bag of groceries while she unlocked the door.

She gave a sudden "*oof*" of surprise at my appearing like that and then grinned. "You are just in time, J.T. I could sure use a hand with all this stuff."

I have never seen so many groceries go into Margaret's house. They smelled good, too, the way that groceries should—a mixed-up smell of apples and celery and brown paper. When I came in with the last load, a five-pound bag of flour, Margaret had flopped down in a kitchen chair and was fanning herself with the morning paper, even though it was winter and snowy outside.

"You would think I was getting old or something," she said with a little laugh. "That shopping really wore me out today."

My news was so exciting that I couldn't possibly sit down. But I had to wait until she finished talking. "As soon as I stow these away we will have a tea party," she went on. "This old bird needs it."

"But first I want to ask you something," I said breathlessly.

She nodded. "Sure thing, J.T. How can I be so thirsty? Would you draw me a glass of water just so I can get my wind back?"

I took down a glass and rinsed it and handed it to her all filled up with cold water. She drank it right down and handed it back to be filled again. That time she only took a little sip before setting it by her on the table. Then she smiled up at me. "Now what is your big question?"

"It's not a question," I told her. "It is an invitation. For the first time in my whole life we aren't having a bunch of relatives for Thanksgiving and Mom and Dad and I want you."

I hadn't even finished and there was already a funny, distressed look on her face.

94

"For Thanksgiving dinner and the day," I went on. "Won't that be fun? Dad likes to watch football the way you do and we'll have a fire and roast chestnuts and play games and have two kinds of pie."

I knew I wasn't getting the invitation out right or she would stop frowning like that and say "yes" really fast.

Something was so wrong that she started to stand up. But her tiredness wouldn't let her. She slumped back down and fiddled with the glass of water in front of her.

"Oh, J.T. Honey," she said slowly, "I would just love to. You must know that I would love to more than anything. It is the sweetest thing in the world for you to ask, but I can't."

"Can't?" I asked, unbelieving.

She nodded. "You have to understand. I have already promised."

"Promised who?" I asked.

"Well," she began slowly. "The new people next door, Duke and his dad. They are having their first Thanksgiving dinner together since the divorce and it seemed to me that it should be more special than a restaurant meal. I asked them over here for a real old-fashioned Thanksgiving dinner." She waved her arms at the kitchen full of groceries. "That's what all this stuff is for, to cook a real old-fashioned Thanksgiving dinner."

I was still standing by the sink where I had gotten her water. While she was talking I stared over at Number Seventeen. Mom had been right. You could see everything from that window, the side of the house and the

95

back yard and right into the breakfast room where the back door was.

"It's really important for this holiday to be special for Duke and his dad," Margaret repeated. "Barkley Street means a lot to the two of them. Duke thinks maybe, just maybe, that his mom is considering letting him come to live with his dad for good. And Barkley Street has done it, the house and having all the kids to play with and this being such a friendly street."

I barely heard the clatter of the yellow van driving in but I knew it was there. I saw the light come on in the kitchen beyond the hedge. I wasn't even thinking of Mr. Garvic. I was just staring, trying to find something to say back to Margaret whenever she stopped talking. Then, as I watched, Mr. Garvic opened his back door and stepped just inside it. I could see his mouth moving as if he were talking but there was nobody there. Then he smiled. Then he stood up straighter and braced himself with his arms out.

A dog hurled himself against Mr. Garvic's chest with enthusiasm, tail wagging and body squirming every which way. Mr. Garvic held him in his arms, laughing. The dog was straining to lick his face, getting its ears all tangled in Mr. Garvic's beard, telling him hello in all those dog ways.

My breath came hard, like a thump in the stomach. That dog was Stilts. He was a lot bigger and fatter than he had been even a little over a week before when I had seen him last. His hair seemed thicker and curlier than I remembered, but it had to be Stilts. Stilts was okay!

96

At first that was all I felt, just a warm flow of relief that Stilts hadn't been hit by a car or put to death by the animal refuge people or frozen stiff in the cold and snow. He had been there safe all that time, hidden inside Number Seventeen and growing healthier and more beautiful every day.

But why? Why would they keep a big healthy animal like that inside and not show him off the way I would have if I could, back when he was mine?

Then I remembered: no children, no pets. Maybe Mr. Garvic figured that he could get away with a boy over weekends, but showing off a dog was too dangerous. After all, Natalie's ''spy'' lived right across the street.

And my letter had been written and mailed, a really unfair letter trying to get the Garvics chased out of their house! I counted the days in my mind. The letter had gone airmail. It was already even time for me to hear from Natalie, and the real estate agent to hear from her father.

Natalie's last letter had made me mad enough to admit to myself that not only was I a fool but she was a troublemaker. And here I was, the worst troublemaker of all. Duke Garvic had called me a spy and Steve Jarvis had called me a stooge. I was both those things and more. I was what my dad calls a card-carrying fool to do and say all the things I had done to keep the friendship of somebody like Natalie.

Not only had I hurt the Jarvis boys that long time ago but I had also destroyed Duke and his dad and my own precious Stilts with my meanness.

Margaret was still there behind me talking about how

sorry she was and asking if maybe we couldn't plan it for another time. I turned and leaned against her just the teeniest bit because she is old and old people aren't safe to lean on. But I wanted to feel her close because very soon she was going to hate me, too.

"Maybe another time," I repeated dully, the way Mom does when she misses a chance that she knows very well is never going to come again.

Mom was really disappointed when I told her about Margaret.

"What a nice thing for Mrs. Cellini to do," Mom said. "That's a lot of hard work and she is not just a girl, you know. It was awfully late for us to extend an invitation for such an important holiday dinner. Maybe another time." She shook her head after a minute. Then she sighed. "Your dad is really going to be disappointed."

I knew why she sighed. We both knew how hard it was for him to accept that Barkley Street wasn't a friendly street like Donaldson Street where he grew up. He had given up on there being a Barkley Street Six-pack of kids that played and grew up together, but it hadn't been easy for him. I have always known that he and Mom blamed Natalie and me for some of the unfriendliness of the street. How would they feel if they knew the rest of it, about the Jarvis boys and the skate and how Natalie let a simple accident cut us away from Tracy Ellis and Mugs?

I don't talk to Mom as easily as I do to Dad but, even if it had been Dad there, I still couldn't have said

98

what was on my mind. They wouldn't have much to be thankful for if they knew their precious Jane was a stuck-up snob and a stooge and a spy with all the sturdy courage of a bowl of unset Jello.

"Maybe another time," I echoed weakly.

11

The Good Old-fashioned Thanksgiving

Well, Mom and I were both wrong about Dad's just being disappointed. Dad had given up on me and Barkley Street so many times that he must have used up all the "giving up" he had. When Mom told him about Margaret not coming and why, he looked off into space a minute, then turned and walked out the door without even putting his coat back on.

It was funny. He was gone a long time but Mom and I didn't say anything, we just waited. Then he came back, rubbing his hands together and grinning like a leftover jack-o'-lantern.

"That's that," he said briskly. "We are going to have a real old-fashioned Thanksgiving after all. You'll see."

"I would be delighted to see," Mom said tartly. "If you would just tell us what you are talking about."

"I've organized this dinner for you girls," he explained. "We are all going to have Thanksgiving dinner together over here. I told Mrs. Cellini that our turkey was already ordered so she should cancel hers. And that you had the pies and rolls already made."

"Then she is coming?" I interrupted.

"Never interrupt a master planner lest he get his train of thought derailed," Dad cautioned me, going on. "Mrs. Cellini is bringing two kinds of vegetables and some apple salad that she claims our daughter particularly likes."

"Wow," I broke in again, because I know that salad. It is full of walnuts in big pieces and red apples with the skin left on and not too much celery. It isn't the easiest thing to eat with braces but it is worth the effort.

He held up a warning hand. "And the Garvics."

"The Garvics?" It was Mom who interrupted that time.

He nodded. "The new people in Number Seventeen. They are bringing those things that men manage best, canned cranberries, pickles, olives, and, of course, nuts in the shell for after dinner."

"Honey," Mom said, reaching up to catch him by both ears to hold him still for a kiss. "You are a wonder."

He winked at me over her head and said, in an aside, "This woman is a slow learner."

The old master planner, as he called himself, had even set the time. Mr. Garvic was going Thanksgiving morning to bring Duke back from his mother's house. By setting the meal at two, he would have plenty of time. This hour, Dad further explained, would leave time for digesting and football and possibly cold turkey sandwiches before bed.

You can imagine how half-and-half I felt about that day coming. I still wanted Margaret more than anyone in the world, so that part was fine. It was also super to see Dad bouncing around as if he had invented the first Pilgrim feast ever. But then there was Duke Garvic. I hadn't spoken to Duke Garvic since that first day in his back yard when he had been so mean and threatening.

Now he had Stilts. I was half-and-half about that, too. Duke had come onto my street and made friends, even started a domino tournament with Margaret. For him to have my dog, too, seemed somehow unfair. But I kept reminding myself that Stilts now had what I wanted for him the most in the world, a home and people who loved him, and I should be grateful for that. It helped to remember how Mr. Garvic looked when he caught Stilts in his arms that night in the kitchen. He loved Stilts just the way I did and that made it all right.

Sometimes it is handy to be known as a shy person. Nobody would expect me to fall all over myself making talk. I wouldn't have to go out of my way for Duke. I would just wait and let him do things his own way and be quiet.

Promptly at two, Dad and I went over to help Margaret carry her stuff. She sure had a lot of things, casseroles and the salad in a big crystal bowl, and the tin she always keeps her cookies in. She was dressed in a skirt and had on nylons instead of ankle socks and her hair was curled extra. She admired how Mom and I had set the table and the place cards I had made. Then, since there wasn't anything more to do until gravy, she watched football with Dad.

By three o'clock everyone was watching the windows, wondering when the yellow van would return with Duke and his father. Margaret rose every once in a while to stare across at the empty driveway of Number Seventeen. "I'm sure they understood it was two o'clock," she repeated every time.

"There's always extra traffic on the roads on a holiday," Mom would remind her and pass the peanuts again.

The turkey was out and cooling. I cut folded paper to make ruffles for its legs while Mom and Margaret tasted the gravy and frowned at each other the way people do when they are deciding about salt. Mom was wondering out loud about putting the rolls in to heat when we heard the familiar grind of the yellow van coming up Barkley Street.

In no time at all I heard Dad talking with Mr. Garvic at the front door.

"We sure are sorry to be so late," I heard Mr. Garvic say as he shook hands with Dad. "We had so much stuff to load up that we almost never got through." His broad grin made it hard to believe that he was sorry about anything at all. Duke was grinning the same way as he leaned back to balance the basket he was carrying with both hands.

"You might as well carry that right on out to the kitchen," Dad told Duke.

103

Duke took a couple of steps before stopping to look back at his dad. ''Don't tell until I get back.''

''Tell what?'' Margaret asked instantly as Dad took Mr. Garvic's jacket. Mr. Garvic just grinned at Margaret and nodded his head toward the kitchen where Duke had gone.

''It's Mom,'' Duke himself answered from the doorway. ''She had Dad over for breakfast and the three of us had a good long talk. She has a great new job she likes and she's not going to have much extra time for a while.''

Margaret couldn't stand it.

''You are going to stay,'' she almost shouted. ''You get to stay here on Barkley Street.''

Duke didn't seem to care that she had guessed his news before he got it all out. He just said, ''Right,'' in that hard firm way that boys do and grinned over at his dad.

''That's just wonderful,'' Margaret said, putting her arm around Duke like she does around me. My mom and dad both looked a little confused.

''We had a custody problem,'' Mr. Garvic explained. ''Duke has been living with his mother and she has agreed to let him move in with me now.''

''It was our house that mostly changed her mind,'' Duke said. ''As long as Dad just had an apartment, Mom wouldn't even think about it. But now that he is in a real neighborhood with Margaret and all, she changed her mind.''

''Margaret?'' Mom asked, still confused.

''Mrs. Cellini has offered to be our standby,'' Mr.

104

Garvic explained. "She will let a housecleaner in and out and be there if Duke needs something after school. Duke and I will handle the big projects the way you folks do, on Saturdays. But this way there is someone on tap if Duke gets sick at school or something."

"Like getting a basketball caught in his braces and needing an orthodontist?" Dad laughed with a sidelong glance at me.

"That sort of thing," Mr. Garvic agreed, grinning.

Margaret got the guest of honor chair at Dad's right with Mr. Garvic next to Mom. That put Duke catty-corner to me so I didn't have to look at him straight. Everybody talked a lot except me, but then I generally don't in a crowd. They ate a lot too, but I could barely get my first helping down.

My letter had been in Germany long enough for Natalie's father to have the Garvics thrown out of their house any day now. The stuff that Duke and his dad had packed in the yellow van would all have to go back to his mother's house. And where would Stilts go? No wonder I couldn't swallow.

Margaret insisted that she wash the dishes with Duke and me to dry and put them away.

"It took me a while to figure out that Jane Todd and Margaret's J.T. were the same person," Duke said, handing me a stack of dried plates.

"Maybe they really aren't," Margaret said mysteriously.

When the grownups were all settled by the fire, Duke looked at me.

"I guess you want to play a game or something," I said.

105

"What makes you act like that?" he asked. He didn't sound insulting, only curious, but I felt my face redden.

"Like what? I only asked if you wanted to play."

"You know what I mean," he said. "Using that tone that doesn't give anyone a chance."

"I'm sorry," I said, because I really was. Then I said it better. "I'd like to play a game, wouldn't you?"

When he grinned his braces really gleamed. "Yeah," he said.

He whistled when he saw the stack of games and puzzles in the music room. "This looks like a toy store," he said, reading the names on the boxes.

"Natalie gave me most of them," I explained. "They were only allowed to take a certain amount of stuff to Germany."

He turned away from the stack of games to look at me thoughtfully. "What was she really like?"

"She was my best friend." Only after my words were out did I realize how defensive they sounded and that I had spoken in the past tense. She *had* been my best friend, and somehow it didn't hurt to know that it was over.

"I know that," he said in a kind of patient way. "But I hear a lot about her that I don't understand. I'm just curious."

I had to look away to think clearly. "She's really pretty, with dark thick hair and vivid coloring." (Vivid had always been Natalie's own word for herself.) "She's very peppy without liking athletics and she's very strong."

"But not athletic?" He was confused by that.

106

"Just strong strong," I floundered. I felt my cheeks flame with color again. "It's hard to explain because you see people differently when they are away."

"I know that," he said again, waiting.

"Natalie's noticeable. She was Track Queen even though she was new. The teachers liked her even though she never made top grades. She liked to be in control." I faltered. "Somehow she doesn't much care how she gets that control."

His eyes were thoughtful on my face. "Did you like that about her?"

"Like I said, you see people differently, maybe clearer, when you are away from them." I was fluttering inside from what I was having to say. Lucky for me Carson, who hates company, chose that moment to get brave and come looking for me.

He stalked right past Duke as if he were invisible and came to rub his whiskers against my face, purring that loud way and leaving my cheek all wet.

"Hey, wow, some cat," Duke said, leaning toward him. "What's his name?"

"Carson," I said.

Duke's face split with a wide, delighted grin. "That's neat, Kit Carson. Really neat."

Duke Garvic would never know how many points he made with me right then. People always ask what my cat's name is but not very many figure out why he is named that. If they say anything at all, it is usually something about a TV star. Duke made points with Carson too because, when Duke reached out to pet him,

Carson arched his back against Duke's hand instead of flinching away and switching his tail that cross way.

"He's great," Duke said, stroking Carson firmly the way Dad does. Watching him, I could just imagine him petting Stilts. But he wouldn't know to call him that. It was strange, sitting there and knowing about his dog, knowing his dog longer than he had, and neither of us saying anything about him.

"I like dogs too," I told him.

"Yeah?" he asked, his head coming up swiftly. "Me too." I could tell he wanted to say something more but he stopped himself.

"We better get to our game if we're going to play," he said, pulling the Ouija board from the stack. "Does this thing work for you?"

"It worked for Natalie," I told him. "But I don't believe in magic."

He grinned. "Neither do I but it's fun to fool around with as long as you don't get hooked. Dad and I have made a big gamble. Let's check and see what the Ouija says about it."

He set the board up between our laps. Carson switched away angrily and jumped on a chair arm to stare greenly down at us. Duke was good with the atmosphere stuff the way Natalie was. He sat up very straight with his eyes closed and asked his question in such a low, spooky voice that little hairs came up along my spine.

It was so quiet in the room that I could hear my own breath and the faint sigh of the furnace shutting itself off. I had expected some really spooky question but he only asked, "Will Dad and I win our gamble?"

For a long time nothing happened. When I sit still I always itch. This time it came behind my left knee and I was aching to lean down and claw at it.

Then very slowly the little board began to move.

It quickened and practically skidded over until it spelled "Y-e-s" as plain as anything.

I jumped when Duke yelled out, and his father cautioned "Hey, there," from the next room.

He didn't explain what the gamble was and, since I didn't have any questions I wanted to ask, we set up a word game.

"Hey, you're good at this," Duke said after I formed some words that he wouldn't accept until he looked them up in the dictionary.

Then Duke's dad was standing in the door.

"Go on and finish your game, Son," he said when Duke looked up at him. "I just have a question for your friend Jane."

While I was making my move, Mr. Garvic took a small folded piece of paper out of his wallet.

Then he held out his hand. In the middle of that paper lay Natalie's gold ring with the genuine garnet stone in it, the ring she had accused Tracy of stealing and I thought little Mugs had dropped down the plumbing or something.

"Duke found this," Mr. Garvic explained. "He was cleaning out that dark hole under the breakfast room and found it along with some old discarded stuff. It

109

looks like a pretty nice ring. I hoped maybe you would know who it belongs to.''

Mom had joined him at the door. I was glad she spoke first.

"Why, that's Natalie's ring. She used to wear it all the time when she first came here.''

I nodded, unable to say anything. Mr. Garvic held the ring out to me. "Would you mind sending it along to her, Jane? I don't even have their address since I have worked only through their real estate agent. I'll pay the postage.''

I nodded and let him put the ring in my hand. Then Margaret seemed to have her casseroles and bowls together and the Garvics were helping her across the street and Thanksgiving was over. I must have gotten to the door someway because, when they reached the other side, Duke yelled back at me.

"Hey, J.T., Steve and Gerry and Tracy and I are going ice skating at the park tomorrow. Come along.''

"And then to my house for cocoa and cookies afterward,'' Margaret added from Mr. Garvic's arm.

"That sounds like fun,'' Dad said, looking down at me. I knew what he wanted me to say but I couldn't do it. Not after that letter I wrote to Natalie, not with the genuine garnet ring burning in my hand.

"Thanks for asking,'' I called back. "I'll see.''

The ring was just as pretty as when I first saw it on Natalie's hand with her fingernails painted the same dark rich red. Looking at the ring caused a dull pain in my chest.

Sometimes when I have done something really stupid

110

and felt terrible about it, Dad has come to put his arm around me. He always whispered, ''Dawn comes a single ray at a time, baby.''

Since Natalie's letter, I had let light dawn on me that way. Anger and hurt and self-pity had all been part of my seeing. Having to face how I had lied to myself, what Natalie had been to me, was hard enough taken a little at a time. But the worst of all was this ring coming like a full blast of searing light that started hot tears behind my eyes.

Nobody in the world could have or would have thought to throw the ring back into the dark place but Natalie.

The tears I fought back were not even angry tears. I was past being mad at Natalie, or even at myself. Tracy was all right, and I would be all right in the end, but what ever was going to happen to Natalie?

I buried my head against Carson's soft, throbbing side. He stretched a curled paw out to touch my wet face.

''Poor Natalie,'' I told him in a choked whisper. ''Poor, poor Natalie.''

12

A Square Red Envelope
for J.T.

Dad said the mince pie ruined his night's sleep. I hadn't eaten any mince pie and I woke up feeling as if my head had been walked on all night. The thing that bothered me the worst was knowing that for once I had all the balls in the air and could have juggled them just fine if only, *if only,* I had not written that mean, terrible, lying letter to Natalie about Duke and his dad. I felt dirty inside even after I had my shower and washed my hair and dressed so that every stitch I had on was fresh from the drawer.

Somehow I had to stay busy. I cleaned my closet, throwing away all the magic things I had collected in my boot box, all the spells, and the fortune strips from the Chinese restaurant, even the paperback books Natalie had given me. I threw away all the letters I had written to her but not mailed, and the letters she had sent me. I kept the leftover dog food to give to Duke later and I kept the box of poems I have been writing since I was in the second grade.

But I didn't feel any better.

It was that garnet ring.

I emptied my collection of locust skins out of a jewelry box and packed the ring in cotton from the first aid kit. I addressed it to Natalie and got it ready to mail.

I couldn't just send it off without any explanation but it was hard to think what to say to Natalie about the ring.

If I had been mad at her there were lots of ugly things I could have said. About how pitiful it was for anyone to be so mean when they didn't have to be. About how silly it was to fool around with magic when there were regular open ways to manage your life. About how sad it was to pick friends only because they were weaker than you and could be controlled.

Like slaves, Duke had said.

Thinking of Duke reminded me of the night I thought I had a premonition about Number Seventeen. Maybe that was the first flash of light in the dawning of my understanding of Natalie. But it wasn't magic. Time had made the difference, giving me a chance to see myself clearly for a change. Maybe I clung so tight because inside I knew the friendship was not forever, the way she said. And sure enough, there was already a new girl in my place. I felt sorrier for that girl than I did for myself.

I printed the letters carefully because this would be the last note I would write to Natalie. "My premonition," I wrote, "must have been about finding this ring." I signed it "Best wishes in the future, Jane."

The postman came just as Dad was calling me to lunch. Dad sorted the mail at the table, handing the household bills to Mom and keeping the envelopes with his company's name by his own plate. He handed me three things, a postcard, a square white envelope, and a square red envelope.

The card was to inform me that choir practice had been postponed because it fell on Thanksgiving Day. The white envelope held a Thanksgiving card from Aunt Beth, who always sends me cards on those holidays that nobody buys cards for.

Mom filled my milk glass and looked at me.

"We're not in such a hurry that you can't read the rest of your mail," she said. "Isn't that red envelope from Natalie?"

I nodded, hoping she couldn't see what a sick dread I got from looking at it. With both Mom and Dad watching me like that, I had to open it.

When I couldn't get the corner pried up, I put my knife in the end and slit it open the way Dad does his. He blows into the envelope to make it open wider. I didn't do that. I just pulled out the folded sheet and began to read.

Time was very strange suddenly. It was as if the minutes slowed so that I was conscious, without looking, of Mom's passing a plate to Dad, of his frowning concentration as he took just enough cranberry sauce to go with his turkey sandwich.

Reading the letter I could hear Natalie's voice speaking slowly behind the scrawled words. I listened as I read, waiting for her to say the awful thing I knew was coming about Duke and his dad being given notice to move away from Barkley Street.

"Dear, dear Jane," it began (just like always). The letters looked uneven and awkward as if she had written in a hurry or with her mind on other things.

I am writing back in a hurry because I have such great News. [The great was underlined three times.] We are going to Munich for the holidays and Carolyn Ann gets to come with us to keep me company when my parents go out.

I am getting so I can speak German better than any of the kids. I can even talk to natives without saying *vass iss* and all that. For the holidays Mom got me a red velvet dress that is just my color with lace around the neckline almost low enough to show off my figure. It is so pretty that you wouldn't believe it.

Hope you have a happy Christmas and go to lots of parties like I will.

Your best friend,
Natalie.

I finished the letter before I saw the little arrow. An uneasy rush of hope made me breathe funny. She still hasn't got my letter, I thought numbly. Could it have gotten lost?

Then I turned the sheet over.

115

The postscript was written in all capital letters:

"It's okay about the hippie and his kid. My folks decided to sell the house anyway and those people made my dad an offer he couldn't refuse. Sorry I won't be coming back but Mom says I wouldn't be happy there after traveling abroad and all." Then there was "Love" again, and the big letter N.

Dad looked at me curiously as I had trouble getting the letter back into the envelope.

"Something wrong, Jane?" he asked. "You look as if you had suddenly been turned to stone."

"Nothing really," I began. "She told me about going away for Christmas and her new dress, and parties." When I paused for breath, my throat felt tight.

"And they aren't coming back. They are selling the house to Duke and his dad," I added in a rush.

I saw the quick look pass between my parents as Mom laid her hand on my arm. "I know that is a real blow, honey," she said.

I shook my head. "It's all right, Mom, it really is. This way Duke and his dad can stay together the way they planned. And like Natalie says, it wouldn't ever be the same again anyway."

"Garvic told me he had gambled on making an offer to Lowery," Dad told Mom.

"Do you suppose they know their offer is accepted?" Mom asked.

"Probably not," Dad decided. "The sale will go through the agency here. You should probably keep this under your hat, Jane, and let them get the news through regular channels."

116

"I'll wait to let Duke tell me," I said, picking up my sandwich. Then I laid it back down. They both looked at me curiously, waiting.

"On a count of three, everyone who doesn't want to see a kid do a home tonsillectomy will shut his or her eyes," I announced, reaching up to pull my bands out.

They both laughed, but they did shut their eyes.

I was giddy that it was all over. I didn't have to dread seeing a red envelope come. Duke wouldn't have to pile his stuff back into that yellow van to go back to his mom. I wouldn't have to face Margaret when she found out how mean I had been. Best of all, Duke would be able to let Stilts out of hiding. Boy, would it ever be fun to have that great lovely dog prancing up and down Barkley Street. Carson would have to take to the trees for sure.

I had started eating my second sandwich before I realized that I didn't have a best friend any more. I didn't even care.

Lunch was just over when the doorbell rang.

Duke's nose was red from cold under his knitted cap. His scarf was long and wide with fringe that hung down like a caroler's. The other kids hadn't come up to the porch. They all stood together in a little tight bunch on the other side of the crabapple tree, just watching.

"Hey, J.T.," Duke said. "You don't happen to have an old pair of skates that might fit Mugs, do you? He has it in his head that he can learn to skate, too."

Dad, behind me, answered right off. "There are some

117

of Jane's outgrown pairs in the garage. You kids come in and we'll see what fits.''

Everything changed just that fast. While Dad went off to the garage every kid on Barkley Street was suddenly right in the middle of our living room. Tracy held Mugs's hand and Steve and Gerry were dancing from foot to foot from cold.

Dad was pretty slick. He just brought my skates with the others and handed them to me before he knelt down to try the smallest set on Mugs.

I barely had time to get my thermals on under my jeans and find my pink sweater before Mugs was fitted up. Mugs grinned, showing a black-looking place where he had lost a tooth. Duke was ear-to-ear silver just like me. We really looked funny standing there together.

Mom cautioned me about my top button as we started out. She never admits to being superstitious but she believes all colds come in through top buttonholes and going to bed with wet hair is the cause of pneumonia.

Dad stood in the doorway with his arm across her shoulders as we started down the walk.

''Well, there is finally a Barkley Street Six-pack,'' he said contentedly, grinning at all of us. ''Long may it wave!''

''Long may it wave?'' Duke asked in a low voice, looking at me with a puzzled expression.

I hopped an extra step to catch up. ''You'll learn about my dad. He is great on slogans and stuff like that.''

Later, when I knew Duke a lot better and he knew me, when Stilts was able to play outside with the rest

118

of us, I would maybe tell Duke about knowing that Number Seventeen was his house even before he heard it. Maybe I would get up courage enough to tell him that I was the one who kept Stilts under the porch and how I had first seen him cowering in the flash of light and all. But there was going to be lots of time for that when we got to be better friends.

The Jarvis boys raced each other to the bottom of the hill and landed in a pile of snow. When they started punching at each other just in fun, Mugs tugged loose from Tracy and ran down to jump on both of them.

Duke and I caught up with Tracy, who was walking all by herself. She still hadn't looked at me. I felt sorry for her because I know how it is when you are shy.

"I like your ski jacket, Tracy," I told her, even though I have seen her pass the house in that jacket a hundred times. "It sure is nice to see you again."

She looked at me searchingly a minute before replying. "Thanks, Jane, I like your pink sweater, too." She looked as though she might be starting to say something else but Duke punched her lightly on the shoulder.

"Her name is J.T."

"Long may it wave," I said for no good reason. Then I giggled. "The Barkley Street Six-pack. That crazy dad of mine."

Celebrating 40 Years of Cleary Kids!

CAMELOT presents
BEVERLY CLEARY FAVORITES!

☐ **HENRY HUGGINS**
70912-0 ($3.99 US/$4.99 Can)

☐ **HENRY AND BEEZUS**
70914-7 ($3.99 US/$4.99 Can)

☐ **HENRY AND THE CLUBHOUSE**
70915-5 ($3.99 US/$4.99 Can)

☐ **ELLEN TEBBITS**
70913-9 ($3.99 US/$4.99 Can)

☐ **HENRY AND RIBSY**
70917-1 ($3.99 US/$4.99 Can)

☐ **BEEZUS AND RAMONA**
70918-X ($3.99 US/$4.99 Can)

☐ **RAMONA AND HER FATHER**
70916-3 ($3.99 US/$4.99 Can)

☐ **MITCH AND AMY**
70925-2 ($3.99 US/$4.99 Can)

☐ **RUNAWAY RALPH**
70953-8 ($3.99 US/$4.99 Can)

☐ **RAMONA QUIMBY, AGE 8**
70956-2 ($3.99 US/$4.99 Can)

☐ **RIBSY**
70955-4 ($3.99 US/$4.99 Can)

☐ **STRIDER**
71236-9 ($3.99 US/$4.99 Can)

☐ **HENRY AND THE PAPER ROUTE**
70921-X ($3.99 US/$4.99 Can)

☐ **RAMONA AND HER MOTHER**
70952-X ($3.99 US/$4.99 Can)

☐ **OTIS SPOFFORD**
70919-8 ($3.99 US/$4.99 Can)

☐ **THE MOUSE AND THE MOTORCYCLE**
70924-4 ($3.99 US/$4.99 Can)

☐ **SOCKS**
70926-0 ($3.99 US/$4.99 Can)

☐ **EMILY'S RUNAWAY IMAGINATION**
70923-6 ($3.99 US/$4.99 Can)

☐ **MUGGIE MAGGIE**
71087-0 ($3.99 US/$4.99 Can)

☐ **RAMONA THE PEST**
70954-6 ($3.99 US/$4.99 Can)